VENITA BLACKBURN

How to Wrestle a Girl

Venita Blackburn is the author of the story collection *Black Jesus and Other Superheroes*, which won the Prairie Schooner Book Prize and was a finalist for the 2018 Young Lions Fiction Award and the PEN/Robert W. Bingham Prize for Debut Fiction. Her stories have appeared in *Ploughshares*, *McSweeney's*, *The Paris Review*, and *Virginia Quarterly Review*, among other publications. She is a faculty member in the creative writing program at California State University, Fresno, and is the founder and president of Live, Write, an organization devoted to offering free creative writing workshops for communities of color.

How to
Wrestle
a Girl

How to Wrestle a Girl

VENITA BLACKBURN

MCD x FSG Originals

Farrar, Straus and Giroux

New York

MCD × FSG Originals
Farrar, Straus and Giroux
120 Broadway, New York 10271

These stories previously appeared, in slightly different form, in the following publications: *Ploughshares* ("Ambien and Brown Liquor" and "Black Communion"), *The Paris Review* ("Fam"), *Virginia Quarterly Review* ("Bear Bear Harvest™," as "Bear Bear Harvest"), *SmokeLong Quarterly* ("Easter Egg Surprise"), *Los Angeles Review of Books Quarterly Journal* ("Lisa Bonet"), *Split Lip Magazine* ("Smoothies"), *The Spectacle* ("Side Effects Include Dizziness, Ringing in the Ears, and Memory Loss," as "Side Effects Include Dizziness, Ringing in the Ears, and Loss of Memory"), *Electric Literature* ("Grief Log"), *Story* ("Ground Fighting"), and *DIAGRAM* ("In the Counselor's Waiting Room with No Wi-Fi," as "In the Counselor's Waiting Room with No WiFi").

Library of Congress Cataloging-in-Publication Data
Names: Blackburn, Venita, author.
Title: How to wrestle a girl : stories / Venita Blackburn.
Description: First edition. | New York : MCD × FSG Originals, 2021.
Identifiers: LCCN 2021014279 | ISBN 9780374602796 (paperback)
Subjects: LCGFT: Short stories.
Classification: LCC PS3602.L325289 H69 2021 | DDC 813/.6—dc23
LC record available at https://lccn.loc.gov/2021014279

Designed by Gretchen Achilles

Our books may be purchased in bulk for promotional, educational, or business use. Please contact your local bookseller or the Macmillan Corporate and Premium Sales Department at 1-800-221-7945, extension 5442, or by email at MacmillanSpecialMarkets@macmillan.com.

www.fsgoriginals.com • www.fsgbooks.com
Follow us on Twitter, Facebook, and Instagram at @fsgoriginals

10 9 8 7 6 5 4 3 2 1

To all the wild, mad girls

Contents

PART II

Part I

Fam

My lil sister/niece/granddaughter/baby cousin doesn't know that she's pretty, so she asks everybody, one post at a time. Her mom showed up at her high school graduation, no one had seen her in eight years. Mothers like that never know how to dress, too much fake jewelry, fake hair, and a big-ass fake leather purse still too small for all her shame and addictions to everything else. My lil sister/niece/granddaughter/baby cousin went to a costume party dressed as Selena or Madonna or Paula Abdul, just a thin layer of 1985 draped over her tits. She works out, a lot, a pic for the shoulder press, 78 likes, a pic for the dead lifts, 134 likes, don't get me started on the squats. She doesn't like when people take pictures when she isn't looking, when her face is the one we see in the mornings when she can't find her keys or when her phone is silent and black and asleep and dead and she has to wait fidgeting in that space so close to oblivion. They put titanium rods in her back when she was eleven to correct the scoliosis. She used to walk around like a Black Quasimodo: loved and gorgeous. The metal

worked to undo the snaked spine, only a little pain and
constipation from the meds to whip her back straight. Afterward, there came new opportunities, new clothes, new
friends, new hobbies, one after another on a conveyor belt
along with the chance to document it all. Her happiness
was electric, blinking, a ding, ding, ding, ding. Disappointment is oily; it has hair and musk and cracked lipstick. Her
mother never spoke at the graduation, just faded away
into the crowd as per the court orders. They say scoliosis
is common in obese girls, the weight on their birdlike skel-
etons is too much. My lil sister/niece/granddaughter/
baby cousin was popular. One hundred seventeen hearts
for feeding ice cream to a puppy. There are never enough
hearts. Of course the monsters came, the trolls, the online
bullies with their emoji fangs shooting projectile venom
of envy and disgust. We were afraid she would choke to
death on the poison like the white girls on TV, hanging
from closet doors, bleeding out into tubs, but my lil sister/
niece/granddaughter/baby cousin never said even a fuck
you, just kept on. When your own mother punches you in
the chest for reasons too small to see with the naked eye,
the rest of the world has a hard time hurting you more.
Sixty-four lols for flipping off the president. Two hundred
sixteen likes for a poolside bikini pose at sunset. She smiles
into her phone where smiles are brightest, in the light, the
wires, the electricity of us who have become everything
to her because in the machine there is no blood, no bone,
and no fat.

Bear Bear Harvest™

The house is on a twelve-acre lot that Mom Mom thought cozy. She has an aerial view of the land and surrounding home designs to prove that it isn't a corner lot, as if anyone could tell. Corner lots draw too much energy and, like so many things we avoid, are considered bad feng shui. The aquarium is on the southeast wall for wealth. I believe the cousins are bad feng shui, but no one ever says so aloud. Like everything, that too must be in the stars.

We have to entertain the cousins all weekend in honor of Sybil's first Harvest™ like she's going to an unexplored galaxy when it's at the mall. Bear Bear understands my eye on the event completely but doesn't say a word about it of course. We are in harmony. Bear Bear is my actual dad and generally silent on most matters about the house or the neighborhood or the city or the globe, really. He reads. He's earned that luxury. Fatherhood is a motherfucker, Mom Mom says, same joke, same irony,

same spit flying through her gapped teeth. I like to bring
Bear Bear snacks just like she does even though he won't
eat. Cousin Sybil, on the other hand, has not missed a
meal or an in-between meal in her whole life and can't
wait for Harvest™, just grinning her delighted jiggly-
wiggly ass off. Mom Mom is in every way free of sharp
angles and has the neck and enunciation of Nigerian
royalty though we went to the continent just that one
time. DNA results compelled her, forty-seven percent
lineage. We brought back plenty of souvenirs to place
around the giant portrait of my great-grandfather. The
image of him over the mantel is so large it is almost ob-
scene. He looks like a scientist/king/shaman/god; the
expression one of total mischief and self-importance. He
started the Harvest™ idea when regulations for business
reached the peak of disinterest, and he saw a need to heal
those suffering in his communities, so Mom Mom says.
I call her Mom Mom because she almost seems like two
people but also because I think she got jealous of Bear
Bear's double name. She says the word *water* like no one
else. I hear "woo to her," and it sounds like a seduction,
like she's conjuring the very thing in the glass, and I can
tell why no one dares fuck with Mom Mom.

The cousins are plentiful in all the ways, their numbers and size and feelings just roaming through the house
like mad geese, tearing bread crumbs off our asses. I have
to tell the youngest, Tricksie, to respect my personal
space—don't press into my hips like a horny puppy all the

time—but she's cute and round and probably in love with me, so it's hard to be cruel.

I used to be able to tell how many meals Bear Bear has eaten based on the smell in the hallway. If there is too much rot from untouched strawberries and pastrami he is on one of his trips, meaning he went so deep into one of those silly books he forgot the basics of life. One time I saw him leave the office for the bathroom, and the smell had gotten so rough I hurried to clear out the trays while he was gone. There were little creatures and ecosystems of mold just happy as hell on all those plates of picked-over lunches and dinners and breakfasts. I needed two garbage bags. I wasn't quite as swift to exit as I wanted to be when I noticed the book he was reading, but turns out it was just another history book. Bear Bear was being darling and trying to divine the future by looking at the past. Pisces are like that, full of sensitive thoughts and secrets. Mom Mom believes nothing is as prophetic as the heavens, so she charts our lives accordingly. There are horrors and missteps in our history where men are desperate and greedy; the clawing and nipping at each other is far too unrefined for her. Of course I tried to peek, but I was too slow and he showed up. His face reminded me of the saddest woodland creature and all that somberness made me want to stroke his bald head and tell him everything will be fine, but I was nine and too small to reach his head and always had doubt about the future myself, so I just left the room with my back to the walls, dragging his trash beside me. After that

I called him Bear Bear because it rhymed with there there. Some names just stick because they are true even if we don't want or need them to be. Now there's always rot.

I'm old enough to know that most men don't act or think or look like Bear Bear. Even Bear Bear used to be just Bear once. He and Mom Mom went out in public together as a couple, smiled together, reveled in the achievements of normal civilized people, not giving a damn. Now Mom Mom is on a currently unsuccessful hunt for a boyfriend to supplement her relationship with Bear Bear. It is not subtle by any means, and women like her never lose the right not to give a damn. Marriage. Children. Incidental. I think she prefers other married partners. That might be her mistake. The selection process is quite mysterious and cryptic. There was the yoga instructor who never went to a Harvest™ and smelled like rose oil; the clinical psychologist who did not offer any free advice, just seemed overly excited to be there. He left us all uncomfortable. There was the investor with the well-manicured goatee who made eye contact with me for what must have been a second too long and was immediately removed from the grounds. An Olympic swim coach stayed an entire April with bad breath and a higher-than-expected BMI. She let the yoga instructor stay over last weekend. Now his kids are everywhere. Mom Mom insists we call them cousins; it's more welcoming. She looked me right in the eyes, smiling over her coffee, and told me, "Stop frightening them." It wasn't clear if she meant the boyfriends or their children. I wonder if all parents look at their children that way, like incessant nuisances who are marvelous to watch. That shook something in me, a string before then too fragile to pluck but that now rang with a mission. I began to observe them all, the suitors, the cardigans and hard shoes, the pink vests and leather coats, the colognes of birch and sawdust and mint, the thick palms and wide shoulders and razor bumps and nose hair and dry knuckles and wide smiles and big heads and baseball caps and this ability to make a big room feel smaller, feel the floors and ceiling all contract like something frail in a vacuum.

Tricksie is learning geography, so we play games, name as many countries as you can that all start with the letter *A*. After a slow spin of her head around the room, across the portrait of great-granddad (Emperor Wizard), over the high ceilings peppered with masks from Benin and Togo, war relics from the Congo, and tapestries from contemporary textile artists with difficult names, she says, "Africa," and we all laugh. She says it with such confidence and pride that it is heartbreaking. In the way she exhales on the vowels, "Africa," I hear it echo in the room like a ghost, moving in and out of my chest as does my own breath. Africa is a continent, not a country, I tell her. She isn't interested but loves that she has brought us all joy and been the source of such entertainment. Tricksie begins dancing around the room chanting, "Africa Africa Africa Africa," until Mom Mom laughs out a tear and becomes very serious and hushes us all.

"There is a country that is also a continent," she says.

Everyone listens as though a great and wonderful truth might be revealed to them. "Can you guess it?" And she holds a hand out to me, a command, *Shut up, child*, she says with her jeweled fingers, knowing I can answer, knowing she has taken the game from me. I leave.

"It was in the stars," Mom Mom said about her own marriage. Bear Bear the true Pisces and our mother the Leo-Virgo cusp are doomed when it comes to romance, though destined to be the greatest of friends, according to her astrology texts. Fire signs and water signs are not typically compatible, though there are exceptions to every rule. She speaks to me like I'm a hundred. I wish she would at least pretend she was my mother and I her daughter and we could have a calm and maternal energy between us, but she insists upon these perverse sisterly best-friend, girl-let-me-tell-you, wine-doused chats about all things too adult. Still, she believes if there is anything a young Scorpio woman like myself needs to know, it is the nature of men. When Bear Bear was just Bear he took me to my first Harvest™, one he started himself as an extension of the family business. We left the property down the long front driveway, the grass cut and dewy; it rained the night before. I could see my reflection in the tiny domes of water on the car. I asked him what a Harvest™ feels like, and he looked at me like I had startled him.

"Are you scared?" He almost laughed.

I was scared, and I was offended. He laughed outright, even slapped his fat knee. He looked at me again.

"You're not scared. I know it."

After the Harvest™ I felt energized and brilliant, both in my mind and in my skin, as if I shone, as if I were radiating outward. Bear Bear picked me up even though I was too old, but he did it so fast that I could tell he'd been waiting a long time to pick me up like that, and it might very well be the last chance, so I didn't protest while I hung up in the air, and the strangers eyed us in our own moment, some daring to look alarmed, others full of understanding and envy. Eventually I did have to pat Bear Bear's hands to indicate that I needed to return to the earth for all sorts of reasons. He put me down. I stayed in close proximity to a mirror for the rest of the evening after that first trip to Harvest™, marveling at my own symmetry. I heard Bear Bear's voice, "You're not scared," and how wrong he was and how wrong everyone was all the time about me and my body and whatever net of energy inside me generated feelings. I thought there must be something broken because the two never seemed to match. My face and my skeleton could not accurately represent the nest of feelings I had inside, but after the Harvest™ it became even more apparent.

With my mother entertaining the cousins, I go to my bedroom and stand centered in the wall of mirrors that conceal my closet. "Stop frightening them," I say.

Tricksie appears behind me like a mushroom, and I don't notice her until she is there. I jump. Fucking Aquarius. They really are mad as a swarm of gnats. She rams her face into my hip again, then falls on the floor, rub-bing her back on the carpet as she grips her own bare toes.

"Your room is empty!" Tricksie declares, still excited, looking under my bed. It's bad feng shui to store things under a bed. Then Sybil enters. They are all here again, these strange nonfamily creatures, still yearning, still scratching and eating and shitting. I see something in Sybil's face that I hadn't all afternoon. I hadn't really looked at her this whole time. She is terrified. I ask her what is wrong.

"Tell me what it's like. Harvest™."

"Is that all? Well . . ."

Then her father shows up at the door.

"All aboard!" he booms in the doorway.

Sybil stands up from my bed and smiles. Her face cleaned and erased, every trickle of horror made invisible. She has a skill I did not at that age: to will the world to see what you want it to see. Her father, the yoga instructor, has a well-defined chest and growing haunches. Sybil hurries past him out of the room, off to her first Harvest™. He stares at me, and says I look so much like my mother it is almost a trick of light. That sounds pretty to me, so I take a step nearer to him. He quickly turns and leaves. Tricksie is still on the floor, watching it all. She laughs at whatever joke played in her head or at her own father's awkwardness. We smile at each other like there was never a time when little girls were not safe in this world.

Mom Mom and Bear Bear had a big fight once around the time he began to refuse to eat. Mom Mom's argumentative style was to fling objects to and fro; there were sandwiches everywhere, hanging on the ceiling fan, sliding down the walls like gutted fruit burst in halves, their innards naked and ashamed. She left the office in tears, in a disheveled mayhem I'd never seen before or after. I could've gone to comfort her, but she was stronger than the rebar in the walls, so I stayed with Bear Bear. All I know is that Mom Mom decided to sell controlling interest in the family business to some food conglomerate. Harvest™ would be a for-profit entity. To Bear Bear, Harvest™ meant something else; maybe the dream of my great-grandfather was more to him than it was to me, another relic on the walls of my home. He was then already a third of the man I'd known most of my life, arched over the desk, bones rising through his shirt. I put my face on his back and said his name: Bear Bear. His breath only stuttering once or twice.

Sybil is well on her way to Harvest™. I never had a chance to tell her that it is not unlike many clinics she's been to before. There are licensed specialists in pastel uniforms, pleasant lighting, ambient music of bells and strings. The only vegetation is in the oil paintings, identical reproductions for every chain. Sybil will be ushered into a quiet room with a table. She'll have to remove her clothes in the dim light, which is flattering to the asymmetrical waistline she's been developing. In the shadows

of the room are two shrub-like structures, Plasticine and
gray with glowing dots; they seem decorative, but they are
the tools. There's a single mirror that allows the guests to
see their current selves, the hanging skin, elbow bags, and
swollen haunches filled with triglycerides; it's designed to
inspire sadness and isolation and a yearning to end it. The
mirror works both ways. Once the staff see the guest has
disrobed fully and lain down, they can enter. Sybil will be
given a gas to slip her into unconsciousness and all the
tubes and glowing needles from the shadows will be ap-
plied to her body, a gentle ripping of fat and restructur-
ing of her epidermis. All of the leftover material placed in
canisters to be sold to food repurposing plants, so nothing
is lost. The drugs afterward will leave Sybil feeling lighter
than dust in a ray of sun.

Bear Bear doesn't believe Harvest™ is beautiful anymore the way Mom Mom and I do. The two of them
have grown closer again. They are the friends they've
always been destined to be. She is letting him disappear,
drain himself of all things solid, drinking only the water
she calls me to bring, and though she feels it a waste
she won't deny him peace anymore. Mom Mom tells
me that men like him have a disease of the mind. They
don't like how everything is turning out somehow and
see what we can't; it makes them unhappy. I believe her.
I believe her because the expression of tenderness also
came with a command, one that clearly said, *I know you
love him and are full of thoughts, but this will happen to you*

too and you know how to think a certain way and not show it for your own good and there are difficult things crawling about the world that sting and bite and infest and torment and vanish only to be reborn in more fierce and startling incarnations, if we let them.

Biology Class

BUY THE BONE

We didn't even know Ms. Lancaster owned all those animals. Somebody broke into her house and got pics: cages lined with shit, torn-out fur and blood everywhere, all over the floors, inches thick like you couldn't walk in it without a sucking sound every time you lifted a foot. She just abandoned them all. So sad.

On the first day of school, we walked into class and could hear something scratching and smell something disgusting. Eventually we got used to it, the raw, acidic stink of formaldehyde and animal flesh. Turns out the scratching was a bird in a cage in Ms. Lancaster's office adjacent to the class. We all sat a few rows back from the front of the class like always—Vanessa included. When we saw Ms. Lancaster for the first time, like usual, everybody got a little wet and hard for the new teacher, who wasn't a total hag. She wore an ankle-length flower-print

dress over her flat chest and had this soft country at-
titude that made her seem like a baby, a really smart
baby who knew about war and sex and taxes. Ms. Lancaster was tall, thin, sure, but not fit, instead skinny-fat
with carpal tunnel in both hands; her arm meat swung
every time she wrote fast on the board or sneezed un-
controllably. She always wrote fast, even with the braces
on her wrists, impossible-to-read handwriting with even
more impossible-to-understand sketches of body parts,
but we didn't care. This wasn't the kind of school for
caring or trying or being special. Standing out was never
an objective. No one was popular. No one existed beyond personal friends for safety. Ms. Lancaster didn't
get it.

Instead, she learned our names, especially Vanessa's.
Vanessa wore jean skirts and Chuck Taylors with vel-
vet tracksuit jackets that clung to her shoulders. She ran
cross-country so always had some well-defined muscle
flexed unawares or shoulder blades pushed back like
she might sprout wings. Vanessa lived on the edge of
being special but knew how far to go, almost. We had
to draw epidermal layers as part of a homework assignment once. Ms. Lancaster demonstrated on the board
what looked like lasagna or cartoon ocean waves, then
pulled out Vanessa's homework and called her up to the
board, put a long stick of chalk in her hand, and asked
her to draw the epidermis. She did, every layer vivid and
distinct: the stratum corneum, lucidum, granulosum,

spinosum, and basale, each with a specific shape and an implied texture.

"Looks like we have an artist among us," Ms. Lancaster said.

Things got a little quiet. Vanessa's lip twitched back to hold down a smile. She had to dodge past Q, who tried to touch her bare calf on the way back to her seat, but we could tell she felt the change in the room. We all did.

Q always touched girls on the back of their necks when teachers weren't looking. He might blow on a girl's ear until she stood up or made some kind of irritated sound. The teachers always blamed the girls because everything else in the room was still. We never said anything. He never really hurt anyone, so . . . Only big dudes ever sat in front of Q but mostly no one at all until Ms. Lancaster's chart day.

After that skin lesson, Ms. Lancaster introduced us to an ongoing project that she spread out for the year. Truthfully, we could've done the thing in a week, but even with all that time, half of us turned in nothing at all. There were other, more interesting things to occupy our energies than animal scraps. She wanted us to acquire a real femur for examination and eventual display. "It could be pig or beef," she said. First step was to go to a butcher and just ask, because the bones are usually thrown out after the sellable flesh is removed.

"Ask the butcher to cut it in half, the long way," she

said. "You want to see the marrow, the layers, and the artery that feeds blood to the center of the bone."

Ms. Lancaster and Vanessa were still getting along then, getting along very, very well, in fact. Vanessa stopped hanging out with us during lunch and spent her free time in the biology lab. Sometimes we glimpsed her in there petting that bird with a head so blue it looked like an accident while Ms. Lancaster sorted materials in the classroom; reading at a desk while Ms. Lancaster shuffled papers; or typing as Ms. Lancaster leaned over her shoulder, dictating passages to Vanessa probably because the carpal tunnel was being a bitch. They seemed to be getting closer and closer over the weeks, literally, and that's when the photo showed up.

It was a blurry pic of a familiar scene to us: Ms. Lancaster at her computer, Vanessa leaning over the desk, both peering at the monitor, all of it seen through the bio lab window. The only difference between our memories and the photo is somebody did a half-assed editing job and moved Ms. Lancaster's hand to Vanessa's thighs, right under the hem of her skirt. The pic and the joke were pretty shitty but well understood. Vanessa even laughed because she had to, she knew that was the right thing to do. When acid is on the ground, it is best not to fall, best to be patient, step lightly into the crowds, and become invisible again.

Ms. Lancaster of course fell, and the mess was incredible. We saw Vanessa try to go into the bio lab after the photo had circulated, but the door was locked. She knocked and knocked and said Ms. Lancaster's name, but there was no response.

BOIL THE BONE

A day or so after that came the seating chart. It was elaborate and color coded and confusing for almost all of us except for the few who sat down in their appropriate locations without blinking. After some high-anxiety moments of panic, most of us found ourselves in the same places we had always been. Backpacks hit the floor in relief, and feet eventually stopped scuffling around for a home, but in that calm Vanessa still stood. She stared at Ms. Lancaster blank faced and hard for a long time, long enough for all of us to notice and wonder and look at Ms. Lancaster and wait too for an explanation to something we had not yet realized. It was quiet. We could hear the parrot in the office fluttering against its cage like a plastic bag in the wind. Ms. Lancaster never looked back at Vanessa or the class, just shuffled papers, waiting. Then Vanessa turned, walked, and sat down right in front of Q.

"Oh shit," a girl said.

Q already had both legs spread wide and stretched out so far in front of him Vanessa had to step over his left foot just to get herself seated. He leaned over and took deep, obvious breaths. We thought for sure Vanessa would protest. There were empty seats around her, some students never came to class—she could've had any of those. She didn't. Instead, she took off her jacket. That got Ms. Lancaster's attention. Ms. Lancaster dared look incredulous as if she weren't culpable, then peered around at us as if we could make this safe again. She didn't understand. We had nothing to give, no reprieve to offer. We were in rapt attention; her performance stunned, captivated. We pleaded in silence for more, more revenge, more mistakes, more shame, more of her to shake loose before our eyes. We looked at her, and she back at us with equal expectation, as if all of us could feel Q's meaty breath on our necks; we held our breath for what was to come. She gave us a lung, a raggedy sketch of a lung on the chalkboard to gaze at. We counted the bronchi over and over, traced their branches until the clock ran out.

Around Halloween we were supposed to be at the next stage of our big project. Find a pot large enough for our femurs and boil them for a few hours until the heat rendered off all the fat and flesh.

More pictures emerged, Vanessa absent from them all but Ms. Lancaster on full display. An entire account formed online: Biology 101-lolol. The first bunch of photos were all in Ms. Lancaster's office at lunch. She was in all varieties of lonely poses with crudely photoshopped birds in unsavory conditions. There was a bowl full of cartoon cardinals posed like fruit, one bird in Ms. Lancaster's hand as if she were taking a bite. The birds were always in jeopardy: burned in an experiment, chopped up, eaten, and eventually used for sexual purposes. The account lost some attention for credulity's sake but regained steam around the time Vanessa slapped Q on the field.

She tried to, actually. Q always followed her around, doing his creepy-guy routine, which was harmless to us generally, but the whole bio classroom's attention must've confused him. Vanessa was bare shouldered and immovable during bio, no matter what he did, even when he stroked the eraser end of a pencil down her neck. She never faltered, but outside of that room, Vanessa and everyone avoided him. Still, one afternoon Q stood right in front of her before track practice and blocked Vanessa's passage to the field, and that's when he reached to touch her abs. She swung on him, but he caught her wrist and laughed. Then he just walked away.

Ms. Lancaster did not do so well either. Her carpal tunnel advanced, and she gave up writing on the board at all. We watched videos in class mostly and did worksheets or not while she sipped water and kept her eyes on her personal monitor. That's when someone kidnapped her parrot.

PAINT THE BONE

After the theft of her office parrot, Ms. Lancaster's physical deterioration grew more pronounced than expected. She posted flyers with a photo of her missing pet, her personal phone number in detachable strips. It had a name: Elizabeth. Seeing adults in physical or emotional despair always left us unsettled, except when they seemed somehow deserving, fit into the range of they-brought-it-on-themselves like all the stories we're told to justify homelessness.

We questioned those stories when Ms. Lancaster fell apart. She came to class with a shoulder brace as if the carpal tunnel had spread like a virus up her ligaments and through her entire nervous system. After the brace came the bloody bandage around her ankle and the limp. It was as if she were losing fights every day of her life now to some invisible opponent, agile and unrelenting. She still sported the floral-print dresses, but they hung awkwardly and were improperly buttoned. For one class the band of her oatmeal-colored bra showed just under her left arm, contrasting with the pink and black dress. It was all alarming but somehow wonderful. There seemed to be switches on these people, these adults, switches that could be flicked and their circuits thrown into always-escalating, ever-delightful chaos.

One of the final stages for our major bone project involved some artistic flare. After boiling the fat off the femur, Ms. Lancaster recommended leaving the bone in the sun for bleaching, "to make the cleanest canvas." For many of us that resulted in an ant fiasco because the bone had not been thoroughly boiled. That, or family dogs literally ate our homework. Those were good-enough reasons as any to abandon the whole ordeal and any hope for a passing grade. Still, it worked out for some, and our sun-bleached bones were made smooth, hollowed, a fine canvas. There were a dozen different sections to identify and create color contrast from the rest. After the painting came the gloss, a spray-painted finish to preserve the work. In theory we imagined a kind of menagerie would form when we brought our final products to class, something bright and celebratory of all the weird effort we'd put into understanding this particular part of the body. In the end, it was not that.

We noticed what happened to Vanessa after winter break. She stopped coming to the bio lab altogether, stopped going to track practice. She had been slowing down for a long time, so no one was that excited about her in the upcoming season, but no one anticipated her complete absence. She'd been putting on a little weight, but it really showed in the spring. The usual suspect had been thoroughly ruled out. She wasn't pregnant or anything that absolute. She just kept putting on pounds, her muscles quickly atrophying under the swelling fat cells. Q had already moved on to other interests and hadn't been seen stalking her in the halls for a while. No one said anything to her about it. We got it. The things girls do to stay safe have to be inventive, manageable, something that can't be easily taken away, a kind of force field. Vanessa's sacrifice of her symmetry did not go unrewarded.

The Biology 101-lolol account doxed Ms. Lancaster, doxed her hard. Home address, Social Security number,

SAT scores, online dating profile, all public and all less than amazing. She was as clean as she was country except for one thing: her animals. She had a hell of a lot of them. The only thing that got attention was the video of her walking through her living room and tripping over an open cage door. There were walls and walls of tanks with gerbils and ferrets and chameleons but no fish. There were rabbit hutches and cat crates and who knows what other kinds of creatures. The abundance freaked people out, freaked out people we never even knew existed. The comments were as cruel as creative. Strangers threatened to murder her if she didn't clean up her house and put the animals in shelters. They accused her of running a puppy mill, then justified her rape and strangulation and even sent pics of her sleeping, sleeping in her actual bed in her actual pajamas but with a twist, blood and bruises superimposed on her body.

NAME THE BONE

No one expected the outside attention or knew how to turn it off or even considered turning it off at all. We figured Vanessa wasn't responsible. Something had overtaken her. Then she changed schools. We saw it all happen. She would sit in class, staring straight ahead, never acknowledging a question, her homework assignments poorly shaded or nearly blank. Once a whiteboard marker

clumsily fell from Ms. Lancaster's crippled hands and
rolled to Vanessa's shoes. The clatter of the plastic on the
tile thrilled us. Vanessa didn't even twitch. Ms. Lancaster
was forced to walk to Vanessa, kneel down, and reach almost under the desk (we nearly fainted) as Ms. Lancaster
raised her eyes to Vanessa in supplication. Nothing. Not
even a blink and a sigh. Vanessa had it figured out like the
rest of us. It's important not to stand out, not to be seen
among the others for too long, no matter how tempting it
might be, no matter who tempts you into the light. It was
a hard lesson, but she got it after a few small mistakes.

There was that one time before Vanessa stopped show-
ing up for good. Ms. Lancaster grabbed her arm in the hall
right in front of everyone. They hadn't spoken as far as we
knew for months, Ms. Lancaster had already looked like
hell and a half, Vanessa had well-developed cellulite on her
exposed thighs, muscles retreated into the warmth of fat.
They just looked at each other, wordless, but we all knew
Ms. Lancaster was pleading, trying to declare her heart as
less than liable. We remembered how they behaved before they knew we were watching, how easily they moved
around the lab, living without an audience, assisting and
being assisted, content. Now Vanessa waited patiently for
Ms. Lancaster to remove her grip, and that was it. In those
couple of seconds, they danced for us, or so it seemed,
sequined under watery light. They were our tragic opera.
How their song made us tremble.

Right before the semester ended, we had to present

our final bones. The last step was to affix tiny labels on all the differently colored parts. There were no clear grading criteria, so that meant make it neat, and it's complete. Secretly we had high hopes for the final conclusion to this brutish endeavor, feeling like the ancients preparing a sacrifice to the gods. There should've been a required bed of herbs to lay the bones on, silver trays or an altar of alabaster stone, but it was just a cold steel counter etched over the years with penises and profanity of various shapes and lengths. The bones were not glorious, were not brilliant or bright. They were just ham-fisted, dreadful clubs to beat down our expectations. Vanessa had already gone for good, failed for nonattendance.

Ms. Lancaster made it to the end, the very last day, before she disappeared too, never to return to campus. Even on that last day we knew she wasn't coming back. She disappeared the way paper disappears when it's crumpled and wet and becomes so unrecognizable it is not even understood as paper anymore but something else, something to be discarded by those who can handle wet and dreary things. Her glow had been on the decline for a while, and seeing her was like watching something grow in reverse, a plant return to a seed or an old television power down, the light extinguishing from the outside until it comes to a single dot and then gone. Someone must love her somewhere probably. Or not. Maybe not, since she had so many animals to take care of. After Ms. Lancaster made her final exit, Elizabeth showed up suddenly, the bird's blue head swiveling happily, its belly full of seeds. No one wanted the animals to suffer.

It was probably for the best that Elizabeth was nabbed earlier, seeing what a wreck Ms. Lancaster's rental house turned out to be. There wasn't as much blood as people think, really. Some of the animals did get out of their cages and roam free in her absence, others just died from dehydration. Many lived, though, the ones that got out probably, the ones that knew where to look for sustenance, how to hide from threats, how to take enough and leave enough. Those are the ones that always survive. It's a shame they eat each other in the end.

How to Wrestle
a Girl

Option 1: Forfeit. Can't lose if you don't play, though it is technically losing. For a teenage boy in America there is little status in defeating a girl or being defeated by one. Claim a faith-based reason for not participating, which everyone interprets as not wanting to risk an erection. Feel righteous and horny. Gradually lose devotion to the sport and eventually your God.

Option 2: Have nothing to prove. Feel secure in your skill and never underestimate hers. She is your equal in weight and height and you are difficult to tell apart from high up in the bleachers. Be awake. Be cautious. Forget your own name because it doesn't matter in the moment.

There are only two positions: top and bottom. Begin in neutral with a smile. Use one of the four basic grips in wrestling, the butterfly, wrist over wrist, elbows close to the ribs. Use your torso strength to maneuver her to the mat. You are now the top.

It was easy because she was thinking about another face, a body full of hope with bruises and neck acne and how nice it is to be close to her. She was thinking about tomorrow, not about your shoes squeaking in a lunge forward. Continue like this until you are named winner or not.

Option 3: Have something to prove as well as a pre-programmed disregard for women, especially lesbians. Assume she is a lesbian. Hate her body, her hair, and the color of her uniform. Green is stupid.

With a simple attack you are now the top. Beam. Believe you have won and leave yourself vulnerable. Notice your opponent slip out from under you. Feel embarrassed as if you've dropped something valuable like your pants and underwear. She binds you via a Gable aka monkey grip, hand over fist to secure you in an armlock. Everyone is looking at you roll around with what looks like yourself; it is unclear who is the boy and who is the girl and people want to see what you will become, so they can call the winner by name. Remember that girls have lighter bones and wear their weight in muscle and fat. Headbutt the girl with your heavy skull, and hope the ref doesn't see it, hope everyone else does. Watch her wince. Smile, or try but fail to remember how.

Use the S grip, curled fingers only, which requires strength in the knuckles to circle her body while it is hurting. Smell her and yourself, indistinguishable as two lit matches. Lift up as she straightens with hands and feet on the mat like a tent. Slap her arms till they welt, will them to release their grip before the timer runs out and you are named. Notice the size of the areolas through her uniform as you squeeze your forearms around her ribs. Feel the tiny soft ridges. Forget how to get hard. Forget your own name. Be flipped to the bottom position. Land hard on your right elbow.

Find yourself seized by the girl in a ball-and-socket grip, hand over fist, great for choke holds and not great for you. Because of the pain in her head she is not thinking about tomorrow, only this hour and your throat and how soft it is and how it yields so easily under her bones. At the whistle breathe again as the ref ends the match to spare you the act of surrendering and/or unconsciousness. Know your name again.

Easter Egg Surprise

While plopped on his training potty in the middle of the apartment den, my son, lil Benny, threatened to kill everyone in the room. While straining, he spoke in his preschool accent and jabbed a finger at each of his targets.

"I'ma kill you. And I'ma kill *you!*"

Those threatened included me and his grandpa, Ben Sr. Both of us laughed of course 'cause it was super cute like a baby penguin itching to wrestle. Grandpa Ben was now my primary babysitter for lil Benny. My mom had just passed. She was a junkie and a liar and owed me three hundred dollars, but she was good with my kid. Lil Benny's mom was about as useful as his grandma if you ask me, though. I left my dad in the glow of the television to dispose of lil Benny's kid shit. While flushing the toilet there was nothing funny left. I didn't turn on the light, so everything was gray, cold, quiet, and smelled of bleach, mildew, and poop. I thought about the news and

the funeral and the genetic transfer of fucked-up tenden-
cies and wondered if there might be something wrong
with my son.

There were garbled voices in my head for a while,
flashes and whispers all saying violent video games are
bad for kids. So I studied up, read the labels, and dropped
lil Benny in front of a TV without screams of bloody murder and the pop pop pop of first-person-shooter digital
gunfire. In his new game there were just tools and block
men ready to build anything. Lil Benny loved it. After a
week though I wasn't so sure.

Benny stopped cussing and threatening to kill me, but
he didn't say much of anything, just oooohs and grunts
and ahhhhhhhs like the block men in his game. He even
started to copy the stiff swivel of their heads. I could tell
his Grandpa had noticed.

"That shit gon' turn him into a pussy."

I let that slide since my dad still had a lot on his mind
of course about the loss of my mom. Doctors guessed the
years of dirty meth led to the cancer. Many of their friends
still didn't know she was dead. When they asked how the
treatment was going, Dad had a phrase for it.

"Burned it up!" he'd say, and laugh like an ass.

A few were confused/horrified but most knew his
ways and cringed when they realized he meant cremation.
Lil Benny's mom left our apartment to buy some mac 'n'
cheese one night and the bitch never came back, fourteen
months ago. Benny still sees her online, posting pictures.

She bought a motorcycle and dyed the top of her head purple then gray then back to black. Lil Benny used to love her hair changes when they video-chatted, never questioned when she would return. To him, it was normal that mothers left like that into the night or tiny containers.

Games were clearly not the answer, so I found a channel online. At first I was confused and tried to click away, but lil Benny stopped me with a grunt. There were no people on-screen, just a pair of white hands and a basket of plastic Easter eggs. The hands worked slowly to turn the egg around for the camera, creating suspense and shit. Lil Benny leaned in closer to the screen just as the egg broke to reveal its hidden gem: cars, animals, superheroes, popular cartoon figurines, and the one Russian nesting egg that lil Benny gasped over as each egg led to another inside, ending with a final micro race car at its core, which gave neither him nor me any satisfaction. Staring at the disembodied hands moving to break one egg at a time over and over made me feel like I was shrinking, like the oxygen left the room and all the toy trucks, robots, mice, candy, key chains, and stickers birthed into view with a tiny explosion of air from the egg were growing big and heavy as bricks piling around my feet, pressing down on my toes. The videos gave me fucking vertigo, but lil Benny couldn't get enough. He became addicted to them, retreating into the screen whenever I had to deny him a piece of chocolate his grandpa brought over because sugar sent him into a hyper-tantrum, and I would have to restrain him through high-pitched screams of injustice. I had to find something better than those vids, though; there had to be something better to help my son than a strange man's manicured hands popping open plastic eggs all day.

Lil Benny's mom's calls became more and more infrequent after he refused to talk to her that one time. She waited for him to notice the rainbow nest on her head, but he wasn't impressed. He ended the call by touching the red button. The boy can't read but can hang up on a grown-ass woman without thinking twice.

I gave in, gave up, went to the store, and bought a toy football. I figured the only solution was to take lil Benny outside. When I got home his grandpa was playing a video game on the couch and lil Benny was in his room. I could hear him laughing and talking to the screen. There were other voices too, a woman and a man and other kids, so I hurried in to see who the hell was in my apartment. Benny knelt at the TV, watching a family online, playing games together in their home. Lil Benny waved a hand at me and said, "Hello, Daddy," without looking in my direction. He said every syllable, sharp as ice. I said, "Hey," squeezed the foam ball, then left. The family in his video sat close. The room was warm, clean, with a rug, lamps, and pillows. Everyone laughed like they would always be that way in there together.

Inappropriate Gifts

1.

When he was four, Darrell wanted one of those plastic toy cars with motors that kids could actually sit in and drive around. He was already twice as big as other four-year-olds. His mother bought him a remote-control car for ages nine and up. He tried to sit on it, broke it, and cried. The laughter from his mother shaken out like dust surprised them both; they did not see any of that coming.

2.

Ten years later, Darrell's mother chanted along to his music in the halls. Bitch, bitch, bitch, bitch, bitch. Kill a bitch. Fuck that bitch. Slap a ho, his mother sang. Nineties

rap was what it was, a place where women became car-
icatures, big-assed, big-titted ghetto sex mannequins, his
mother claimed. They were sad songs to her, but she let
him have them for the sake of his happiness.

Darrell opened his bedroom door, the beats from his
stereo vibrating the house like a storm. In the bathroom
he ran his palms down over his chest to press the flesh
deeper inside as if the fat, the almost-breasts, were a wrin-
kle that could straighten with pressure. At the breakfast
table, his mother smiled with a faint mustache she removed once a week using a white lotion from the grocery
store. He could tell she skipped her treatment and felt a
warmth toward her that he forgot was possible. It was
pancake Saturday. Darrell dressed and went outside to the
weight bench on the patio for a workout. He counted each
push-up aloud like a poem. Coach let him play football
because he was a boulder even though he couldn't run.
Bad knees. On Mondays, his coach bought him SlimFast
shakes even though he didn't ask for them. Chocolate.

3.

Darrell does not become a rapper or an NFL star, he
gets a government job he hates but keeps it because of the
medical benefits. He marries his daughters' mother, di-
vorces her a decade later, and begins running; it hurts. He
loses seventy-seven pounds, becomes lighter than he ever

was in high school, holds the leftover skin in his hands while looking in the mirror, and wonders what it was all for. His children are like surprise parties, full of wonder and dread and impossible to calculate. He and his ex-wife agree on one last thing. Girls need to know the world—what love is, what violence is, what hate looks like, and how close to each other they all can be. That means boxing classes.

The girls sidestep around the ring nimble as deer, with serious faces often, peeking over the ropes to see what is outside. They are unhappy. They are getting bigger, prettier, and smarter, so this will help them lose a few, ward off male attention, and eventually know how necessary this kind of unhappiness is. He gains all the divorce weight back and a little more because everything is so peaceful until the girls want pop music. They want love songs about teenagers in parts of California he has never been to. He imagines his beautiful, chubby, hairy, dark girls wandering the lyrical sidewalks of those songs and is afraid. While they are walking home together from practice, the youngest sings aloud to a terrible bright sugary tune. Darrell loses his breath and has to stop for just a moment. His youngest tells him he's out of shape.

4.

Soon Darrell will lose twenty years to parenthood, time being the only price it asks of anyone. For Christmas, his daughters will buy him cookbooks for dialysis patients and a smoothie machine that costs more than his car payment. Darrell will forget what he really asked for and remember instead when his mother broke her hip from a fall on the sidewalk, how the ground seemed to suck her into it, the way she stayed there unable to move as if all gravity found her bones irresistible, and he felt an urge to laugh and scream as if she suddenly weighed as much as every woman ever. He will see his daughters swell into their bodies like the seasons.

Lisa Bonet

Okay, so these are the things we have been told never to say in front of children or white people. When I was a kid my grandma used to sprinkle Ajax around the door to keep evil spirits away. It was some voodoo ramajama-type thing mixed in with Southern Baptist rituals. To this day, I got crazy germ phobias and have trouble kissing my wife. Grandma taught me there are horrors you can't see and can't talk about, but that shit is out there. That was the nineties.

Back then me and my wife both had a crush on Denise from *The Cosby Show* as kids. There was this episode where Denise sat on Bill Cosby's lap and she was all eighties cool with rainbow cheeks and postapocalyptic clothes that made her look like a boy who just raided Boy George's closet. She was cool as hell, but even then I thought she looked kinda old to be all on her dad's lap.

I remember when they told us Martin Luther King Jr. was not a perfect man but led a perfect cause. I thought he was bad at math and not bad at fidelity or fatherhood. There were lives at stake so you know you stay quiet. The books back then made slavery look uncomfortable and irrational, something obviously temporary. They never showed us the tools, the funnels to force-feed slaves that tried to starve themselves to death, the spikes driven into the skulls of infants because Black children were thought to be more likely to survive. Why would anyone have to survive that? It took hundreds of dead babies to prove the theory wrong. My wife told me about the old laws that made it impossible to prosecute the rape of a slave because Black women were "lascivious" by nature and of course property. Even when I tell her that's terrible she just looks at me like I don't get it, like no matter how much empathy I can scrape together I'll never know what it's like to be the spectacle of female pain when that suffering is ordained as law, as theater.

Bill Cosby was always Bill Cosby, but eventually Denise became Lisa Bonet, the actress. She got crazy. Everybody thought she was crazy. They said she and Bill had a falling out. I thought then it was because she wanted to be paid more on the show, greedy Hollywood bitch, right? So later when Bill Cosby goes to court for drugging and raping bunches of women, we're all . . .

Today, I want to kiss my wife as often as she'd like, which is too often. She is not strong or proud or wise or witty and is not a perfect best friend. She wakes up too early in the morning, can never find anything, but has good breath. She is not magical, never learned to swim, was severely abused as a child, and is absolutely beautiful like an egg sunny-side up. I am not that attractive I'll admit, but she likes how I think and talk and complain, so we're cool.

When she tries to smash her lips on mine I almost always wince. She tells me I'm traumatized and laughs, but she's hurt, I can tell. It's the bacteria, though. I've seen all the documentaries about good bacteria and bad bacteria and how we need some to live and would not survive as a species or planet without them, but in my head they are large as criminals with teeth like a barracuda's, all invisible and gnawing away. She looks at me when I try to explain about the film on our tongues and I fail to explain and she wants to be patient and not resentful that her childhood looked the way it did and mine didn't and we are so close to understanding each other but can't quite and are left desperate for some impossible thing. I just want her to close her mouth, so I can love her . . .

Live Birth

Nell had three children before she had a say in the matter. Then she had six more. Because she was so good at childbirth and liked to walk between houses deep in the woods even when she had no business at all among the pines, the town made her a midwife. The women there weren't allowed in the hospitals, so they gave birth over straw, standing up, in their own homes. Most of the births were fine, though not all, but every baby smelled fine once the odor of metal and salt was washed away. Nell didn't remember the fine babies, only the others like the one born blind and quiet yet full alive, some stillborn or breech. Another came out backward and hairy as a cat.

One mother made it to the city and saw a film with a woman lying in a bed, giving birth to the devil. Nell too heard stories. There was supposedly a boy born with five hands and no face, his little cries locked up in his throat like bees. But that mother didn't care about bees or the devil or hands piled onto a wrist like petals, just the bed. She didn't want to stand up to deliver her child. Nell told her when fruit falls from a tree it falls down not sideways. Which is easier, dropping a sack of flour or throwing it across the room? The woman just blinked and let her mouth hang open, and Nell thought this must be how the baby happened to her too.

When there were no bellies to check on, Nell still took her walks. Her husband didn't say much but sometimes seized her by the elbow and said, "There ain't nothing in the trees for you." She'd pull away and go on.

Her sons left town and came back. Her daughters got degrees and got fat. The hearts of two sons stopped for good a year apart. She walked between houses through winter and spring for as long as she could, then borrowed a horse until she bought her own.

One baby was born almost a boy and almost a girl, so like God she declared one over the other for the parents to believe forever. Often there were more fingers and toes than ten and twenty. She fixed it for five dollars, tied a string around the extra finger and pulled it tight until it separated from the rest of the hand like clay.

When they took her midwife's license, the mothers in town went to the hospital and paid more money than they had to men who didn't know their names, and sometimes died for all the trouble. Nell divorced her husband, gave her horse to one of their sons, and planted string beans, rutabagas, collards, and mustard greens too. Grandmothers brought their granddaughters to Nell, mostly for good luck. They wanted to know things would be okay.

Nell only said, "My melons don't grow in June like they used to, and the seasons never felt like this before."

There was a birth a long time ago that Nell rarely mentioned but dreamed of often. The mother listened, obeyed Nell's instructions for months, and did her part well on the critical day of labor. In two hours the child was free. When it arrived Nell couldn't give the baby to the mother, just wrapped it up quick, hoping it made no sound, afraid of what that sound might be. When the mother saw Nell's face in the fading light among the scent of sweat and blood and fig blossoms they both knew then how some things expected, longed for, hunted in our minds have been lost to us for a long time.

Thirteen
Porcelain
Schnauzers

Partner #1 and partner #2 believed their *real* sexual dysfunction was because of the dogs: Duchess and Gnarls Barkley. Gnarls was almost ten and Duchess barely three. Four months had gone by since the couple had had sex or had a conversation that lasted more than twenty minutes without fighting or made dinner with both of their bodies in the kitchen at the same time or gone to the movies together or exchanged kinky pictures at work or planned a vacation or anything at all. Partner #1 was long-boned and somewhat feminine in voice and skin care regimens while partner #2 spoke with a husky patience that disarmed everyone and possessed refined abdominal and shoulder definition.

Duchess walked with the elegance of a librarian alone among her books but took to strangers and other dogs like a cockroach when the lights come on: panic. Gnarls

Barkley, however, could not be more graceless, small, close to the ground, or indescribable in breed or disposition. He loved wildly, from his food to the beggars on the sidewalk. All were his, and he was theirs. Playtime between the two dogs was like watching a teenage girl spin an old man around in his wheelchair till he hollered please stop. Partner #1 and partner #2 loved their animals unconditionally.

The website for the trainer seemed legit and even included an interview on a national morning talk show, no pricing info, which piqued the couple's interest, daring them to prove their worth as newcomers to such a high-priced city with unattainable real estate. On their appointment day, the couple walked up the stairs to the trainer's home not at all prepared for what they'd encounter. Drums and chants welcomed them. There were shrines to several gods, some recognizable to the couple and others more mysterious. Partner #1 had seen Santeria in practice at her aunt's home, a Cuban expat with glaucoma and a temper. Here was a familiar altar easily mistaken for an abstract sculpture, wires and scrap metal, the head of a broken hammer, slips of paper, one with a penciled eye, at the center a female doll, Our Lady of Charity, all painfully and meticulously arranged. Partner #2 saw the look of recognition in partner #1 and felt more at ease. A happy Buddha losing small flecks of gold paint rested under a mirror. Beside the mirror hung a tiny Christ like a queer sconce, similar to one that still resided in partner #2's

childhood home, the son of God on his perpetual cross
with tears of blood frozen on his head and ribs.

The trainer led them all, partner #1, partner #2, Duchess, and Gnarls Barkley, out of the hall of deities and into
the main room, where yet another shrine existed. They
noticed a side table without a cloth, laden with figurines
of gray schnauzers in many sizes—one too big for the
top of the table so it sat underneath, others strategically
placed above in various poses of delight, play, sadness, and
contentment. Their clay tongues lolling or pointed, ears
perked in perpetuity. Partner #1 and partner #2 looked
at each other and nearly smiled at the question posed by
this house: What kind of human collects both gods and
porcelain schnauzers?

Silently, the couple shared a thought about the moral-
ity and/or sanity of practicing so many religions at once in
such close proximity inside of one room and one woman.

The couple's reverie was not long-lived and they remembered why they were there, and it wasn't for religion
or a religion that still had a name. Shortly after moving in
together partner #1 touched partner #2's breasts in a way
that was declared offensive. The two have yet to recover.

In the light of the main room, the trainer glowed like
an aging rock star except her feet were bare and toenails
a little dirty. The trainer sat everyone down on a green
king-sized sheet that covered the hardwood, and asked
what were the main issues. Partner #1 considered the
question and how much there was to repair, how they had
tried several cramp-inducing sex positions, how they

had abandoned them all for wine and binge-watching television shows, how soon their lives were consumed with cleaning, washing clothes, and wiping every surface of their home and cars and seeking out exhausting menial domestic gestures of affection to avoid each other but still be with each other, and how touching partner #2 now looked more like calculus than love. Partner #2 said the dogs didn't get along. During the move to the city, Duchess bit Gnarls Barkley twice on the back of the neck for undisclosed reasons. The attack was brief though blood fell.

Both partners #1 and #2 had high expectations for the trainer's response to both the answer given and the one unspoken, and after a serious nod the trainer said, "Well, if they've been violent they can't be alone together anymore; the risk is too great." It was an obvious solution that they hadn't considered, and felt somewhat more hopeful, a kind of relief. An inevitable end for them all: separation.

Then Gnarls Barkley lost his shit. He growled and whined and lunged and humped in the direction of the dog shrine. On the website the trainer wore a sweater with her business logo and jeans. She spoke with a boss-like kindness and authority even to the hostess of that morning show, as if she were being trained along with the labradoodle panting under spotlights. But here in her wide brown skirt with lace trim and the ferocity of Gnarls Barkley, the trainer sweated. She made attempts to control him with odd clicks and snaps then squirts of water and bitters to his face that all failed. Her embarrassment was sour, and could not compete with the feral desire of Gnarls Barkley for every one of the porcelain schnauzers. The partners realized that the relief they felt earlier and the solution given came from a charlatan, that she did not understand how to teach love. They would not take her advice or pay her fee when every promise of a correction lay broken. The couple would go on, drawing blood from barely any contact while waiting for a real answer. Partner #1 spoke gently, excusing them all from the room and the shame, then passing through the hall as every one of the gods closed their eyes.

Not for Resale

DADDY'S GIRL BARBIE

Treat her like she's the best because her daddy says she is his little girl. She plays sports with the boys, rides in the front seat, swears at the playoffs, and starts a gas-powered lawn mower. Daddy's Girl Barbie doesn't need your approval when she has his. Be tough, never feel scared to speak up for yourself. Learn to feel more comfortable in groups of guys than with girls and develop repressed sexual attraction to older men.

Comes with three sports balls, removable baseball cap, game-day T-shirt, and shorts. Two-door Jeep and disregard for the value of women sold separately.

PTSD BARBIE

Imagine loving your country so much you would go anywhere to escape it. Feel the power of semiautomatic weapons and the screams of hot death still not as terrifying as your own childhood trauma. Be everything you can to everybody else because that is the minimum expectation for a woman: soldier, widow, mother, and mistress. Failure is not an option, especially when substance abuse keeps one unaware of time and space.

Comes with Army fatigues, tattered bathrobe, a four-day supply of marijuana, and a stack of unopened bills. Memory of war zone fatality not included.

SEX OFFENDER KEN

Though difficult to spot, he is often included with many Barbie extended-family and neighborhood editions. Comes with removable dad bod and inflated sense of self.

FAT GIRL BARBIE

Know that there are amazing possibilities all around and inside. Never feel ugly and alone, because feelings are edible. Fat Girl Barbie remembers being outgoing and athletic as a child before personal tragedy upset her trajectory. Enjoy a potential for growth and artistic achievement along with a sparkling tendency toward unhealthy amounts of sex with unhealthy people. Never have enough of anything, including alcohol, Fruity Pebbles, anal, onion rings, and BDSM porn.

Comes with Thin Girl Barbie wrapped in outer frame of Fat Girl Barbie + varying degrees of self-esteem issues.

JESUS KEN

Exciting adventure awaits in the historical revisionist minefield of Judeo-Christian theology. Have your image and symbols co-opted by white nationalist agendas. Let's not forget capitalism! Billion-dollar businesses lobby your representatives, catering to the large Christian voting bloc. Offer hope to the most vulnerable communities of color that recognize the beauty of compassion, but not tools that arrest consciousness. Only the best brown leather sandals for the son of God. Most boxes will be empty because the wonder of Jesus is often best left to the imagination.

Skin will darken or lighten under hot or cold water to satisfy owner's racial preference.

BABY DYKE BARBIE

Explore the grief of losing your most understanding and tolerant parent so thoroughly that it ages you half a lifetime in a year. Possess the maturity level of a thirty-year-old before you can legally drive a car. Marvel at your first sexual experience with another girl that is so good you cannot hold your lesbianism in till your late twenties as is expected to avoid bullying, ostracization, and some-times homelessness. Be free in your choice of haircuts that resemble R&B singers' from the late 1990s. Challenge the femme/butch dynamic with an androgynous makeup routine honed to perfection over ten years. Have fewer followers on social media but far more loyal friends than any straight people.

Lace-up military-style boots, lip gloss, and gold chain definitely included. Strap-on sold separately.

TEEN PREGNANCY BARBIE

Transform into an adult in the blink of an eye, then back again. Teen Pregnancy Barbie is actually not one doll but three! Depending on the operator's mood, Teen Pregnancy Barbie can wait a few months and manage a relatively easy birth to become Teen Mom Barbie or instantly become [Your Choice] Barbie. Teen Mom Barbie knows the struggle but relies heavily on familial and government support to survive, eventually transforming into [Your Choice] Barbie.

[Your Choice] Barbie has the largest accessory package of any Barbie because yes, she can be any Barbie.

Comes with Gender-Neutral Baby. Failed Birth-Control Ken sold separately.

Smoothies

The first time a guy said I look like a man was at the Jamba Juice stand in the mall. He was still a boy, probably my age and sticky from adolescence. *You look like a man.* He said it as if he had the right to say anything to me. As if it was important for his survival, an echo of his ancestors who were my ancestors, long and Black and muscled, though we were two strangers holding smoothies. His phone was three generations older than mine. I had superior sneakers, a designer sweatshirt, better moisturizer, and even my drink held more protein and complexity, but he wielded his right to possess them all in one note of disgust. I took a sip as a man in a suit too tall to have a head in my sight line jingled the change in his pocket.

You look like a man. It took a few seconds before I knew it wasn't a compliment, that it was a lesson, an exchange, that he was learning too, how to be a man by not being a girl. In Sunday school we were learning about the first man and first woman and how Adam must've been closer to God because God made him first, and pretty much all

the problems of all time thereafter came about because of
Eve and a snack. I chewed a hunk of ice that hadn't broken
down properly, and a woman hit the headless suited man
in the heel with her stroller.

The boy could've said the words like he'd say *hello* or
nice to meet you or *where did you get that watch* or *what a wonderful day it is to be upright and breathing here together*. But he
said them in a different way, the way we tell strangers your
shoes are untied or you have toilet paper on your ass. He
saw himself in me and felt ashamed. He saw himself in me
and felt proud, but pride wasn't supposed to live inside of
women, so he had to walk it back and cut its throat till the
blood ringed around my neck.

You look like a man. Years later it would become, *You
eat like a man. You walk like a man. You sound like a man.* My
chromosomes had not yet been tested. My birth certificate
says female, live birth, seven pounds and three ounces.

I didn't think I wanted to be loved by boys until that
boy told me it was not possible. I don't remember what I
looked like then, a few years ago, but I remember him, his
dirty Chucks, ashy corners of his mouth, and dry scalp.
Back then I stared deeply at people the way children do,
still curious. He existed. I didn't expect him to look back,
though. Children are rarely seen, but I wasn't a child anymore and had not fully realized that. Now strangers could
assert their judgments on my whole body, my whole story,
without permission.

You look like a man. I was three sips into the smoothie
before it hit. To be a woman seemed a terrible thing to

have happen, and it happened at 3:54 on a Friday when
I was fourteen to the sound of a blender jolted to life.
Women have to be small, give birth, wear makeup. I could
see all the women, the court reporters, the accountants,
psychics and secretaries, biologists and senators, important
but nameless, with inconvenient hairstyles and morning
routines. Men got to invent women over and over one
generation after another by the grace of God.

The woman's stroller spit out a toy from what must've
been a child tucked inside. The mother cooed, then retrieved the toy and fed it back to the stroller. The mall
was not a place to fall apart. It happened anyway. When I
get hurt, usually the universe opens up a little, like a bul-
let through a watermelon. Things separate and scatter.
It feels like this is how we really are all the time and
everything else is just pretend. We pretend to have legs and
skin and penises and milk ducts. We pretend some skin
looks one way while other skin is different. We pretend
to have green eyes and brown eyes and yellow teeth and
gray teeth, and the sky is blue to us in the day and black at
night. We pretend lots of things that are only sort of true
when we are the sky and time and memory and the center
of the earth and destiny and gods and gravity and salted
oceans and children of the gods who ate their mothers
and birthed the constellations and nebulas and death are
a myth because everything goes into itself to begin again.
There was fear and doubt on the boy's face when I finally
turned away. The condemnation dissolved. I, a girl, would
grow to be a better man than he and still be a woman.

The sugar pooled like acid on my tongue when the feeling passed. All the other customers departed, and it was just us under the fluorescent lights together again. There seemed nothing left to prove and a whole new point was born between us that we had not yet named.

Blood, Guts,
and Bile

Nicole gathered her can't-leave supplies for work on set—cordless power drill, color wheel, brushes, assortment of battery-free sex toys, acrylic paint (red, white, yellow, and black), blowtorch, and two packs of chewing gum for the stress. Walking into work was like strolling through a traveling meth den that happened to settle in the middle of a high school production of *Julius Caesar*; it was really coming together, and Nicole could hardly stomach it. There is a great and terrible force that moves among everyone on earth, this viscous invisible fluid of magnetism that is especially heightened in confined areas with poor ventilation and no natural light like subways, holiday dinner parties, brothels, and film studios. Fourteen years trailed behind her in the special-effects makeup business, a seamless pageant of costumes, rubber cement, paint, and body parts held and mashed into variations of glory and dismay. Her space was really just a corner partitioned off in the studio, large enough to house small aircraft but tiny by industry standards.

Nick!

I can't give a single fuck right now, Ree. This body armor is going to take half the day.

Not one solitary single fuck? For me?

Ree was the only man Nicole had successfully fantasized about having sex with, a deep-voiced, super tall, mostly asexual with the build of an inflatable dancing air man, but he could suddenly become that sexy school principal, the captain, the authoritarian smooth as a jazz trumpet player with the unfortunate vocabulary of a twelve-year-old girl and mannerisms of a 1990s R&B singer, meaning he was super gay. Nicole held her head inches from the flame of her blowtorch as it neared the tip of a pink cylinder; the heat forced movement in the plastic, a concave and bubbling hiss. She looked up and said, *What is it?* with her eyebrows, the light of patience and love returning.

Dar is on her way, Ree said, supposedly she tried to call you. She is super pissed, and everybody is seriously envisioning you as one hundred percent fired. I am not even kidding right now. Nicole let her eyebrows lower, shoulders rise, lips pout in a firm no-man-let-alone-a-little-white-puny-woman-runs-my-life-because-I'm-a-powerful-Black-woman-in-full-control-of-my-destiny-motherfuckers sort of way, though her immediate financial predicament, which was her perpetual financial predicament of barely enough to cover rent/food/gas/pretense of having more than enough, meaning never enough to cover rent/food/

gas, meaning a cycle of growing debt and never-ending supplication to the patriarchy and its minions, which was number eight on her list of worst fears right above homelessness and prostitution out of desperation, meaning prostitution, put her in sudden fear of whatever judgment Dar might lay before her.

Nicole's phone is not on the list of can't-leave items, especially since Reginald "Ree" Lee is the only person she ever really talks to, and they work eleven hours a day together. Nicole earned her spot as this feature's special-effects go-to gal when she delivered the base for a set requiring a frozen Medusa. She found a bust of George Washington, sanded down the eyes, melted dildos to the crown, and voilà, a star was born. Dildo Medusa was Dar's favorite prop, but it had been rapidly turning into Nicole's one-hit wonder.

She arrived. If Nicole were a tree, Dar would be the tiny pug that comes to pee on it every day. There was something oddly natural in that arrangement, not because of sex or race or orientation, though it could be argued that Dar was an heiress to a fortune of a certain kind that Nicole still couldn't quite quantify. Dar was short for Darcy, Darcy MacDowell, originally from Shreveport but worked the accent out of her vocal cords with Grey Goose and cigarettes. As with many women of her generation, her aging hormones left her figure asymmetrical like a dented can of stewed tomatoes, and unwillingness to wear a proper bra caused her breasts to float sneakily under her ever-present faded black T-shirts. There was something about

their connection, something Nicole never talked about
except with Ree. They were nearly fifteen years apart,
Dar pushing fifty so hard you could see the digits on her
palms. Nicole was just over thirty and delighted as hell not
to be twenty-anything anymore. The two were the same
height (not tall at all), had a thing for beautiful sexually
fluid women (good Lord, yes), and though they were
working on a sci-fi historical disaster film about zombies
in ancient Rome, they were true artists, who cursed the as-
sumption that computer-generated images were superior
to good old-fashioned latex, and appreciated each other's
profound ability to imagine something else, a better you
than you could ever dream of, a you so powerful that it actually swallows the original, holds it under its tongue to sa-
vor the birth of something bright, new, robust, fierce: the
mangled corpse of a soldier who fought, died, and rose to
fight again in the undead armies bound to the task of re-
trieving Helen of Troy (even though that was historically
a different country).

Fabulous, absolutely fabulous, Dar said with her
knuckles under her chin, just what I was hoping for, incredible, all of it, well-done, well-done.

She departed as quickly as she arrived, oily Converses
squeaking away to the lights and action far, far away from
Ree and Nicole's little corner.

Haa, you're dead, Ree said, so fucking dead, fill out
your unemployment like yesterday, because that was it.

Ree said that loud enough for the nearby staff to smirk
before he winked at Nicole. Everyone knew praise was

one of those things lost in translation in the world of low-
budget special-effects filming, much like vibrators become
the rumbling of garbage disposals and hamburger wrappers become napkins to wipe one's quiet tears upon in the
restroom between takes. Nicole appeared to not do well in
that moment and needed to rethink her entire approach to
the monster destined to compose some of the final shots.

We've got dolls, Nick.

Don't call me that.

Ree nicknamed all cast members "dolls" for fun. He
nicknamed Nicole Nick for torture. She once explained
that he was subverting her femininity for irony when
irony was not yet earned. He responded by grabbing his
genitals and sticking out his tongue and pumping the air
in front of him, a more emotionally complicated gesture
than either of them put words to. Now she just exhaled,
puckered her lips, and opened her mouth slightly around
the drill bit. She read the brand.

Dewitt, she whispered while making the motor purr. I
should do it, she said.

The "dolls," the extras, had arrived and her moment
for mock-suicide theatrics had passed. Ree criticized the
outfits on three of the young women. Today the island of
Lesbos was under siege. The entire horde of Sappho devo-
tees were to fall in a fiery blaze of arrows and arise burned
and steaming for some hot zombie lady lovin'.

You are why I get up in the morning, Nicole said to her
favorite of the cast, Chloe, while waving her over.

This was Nicole's fourth film with Dar, and she always

had a favorite, who was always Dar's favorite. Most of them she couldn't remember because most of them were shapeless, something to turn into something else, a thing that liked her better than Dar, a thing that noticed how she could be more kind, appreciative, attentive. One actually ended in sex, but that's not the one she remembered most. There was Centurion #2 in *Mermaids from Space* who always knew the best burrito spots. Blue horns cascaded from her forehead down to her neck with guacamole at the corners of her mouth. The two laughed hysterically over almost anything. Those were happy days, Nicole thought, with whoever that was under all that rubber.

Today she was with Chloe and Nicole thought she might someday remember who that was. Chloe Chu was not American, not white, which made her somewhat of a cliché, a revolutionary, and an inexpensive commodity. All the new actresses were from across the seas or north of the border for some reason now and very, very young. At thirty-two, Nicole reasoned she must be getting very, very old and no one had told her to stop yet. She and Ree had speculated that the foreign actors were cheaper and could do American accents better than Americans, and talking to Chloe put some truth to that, but since Nicole didn't operate in that end of the business, she could not be certain.

How was your morning, sweetheart? Nicole asked Chloe.

Oh my God, Nick!

Nicole cringed at hearing that nickname Ree made a thing, but continued to mix face paint calmly. The room was cold and industrial, but Chloe's skin was warm, the color of leaves that have lost all their green. Nicole tilted her squarish jaw like turning a camera to find the best angle. It seemed a shame to cover up that warmth and color with cold purple foundation.

I did it, Chloe said with her eyes closed, smiling, her face held gently by Nicole.

You lost your virginity to DiCaprio?

Shut up! Her eyes shot open. I got my driver's license!

Same fucking thing!

They high-fived it. Chloe was a talker, said she hailed from Brisbane, confirmed she was barely drinking age, some kind of East Asian. Nicole imagined a little girl from Chongqing, China, growing up in the outback, doing kung fu with a kangaroo because visually it was cute even though possibly racist. Chloe's face was like a morning where nothing had to be done, just rest, her frame lithe, tall, and she believed in the Los Angeles public transit system for three full years. For that last one she was a marvel and a treasure to both Nicole and Ree.

Where did you go first with this new freedom?

Well . . .

Nicole stopped listening and let the young Aussie's charm fill the room for eighteen minutes where there was once only despondent dread and loathing.

What would you have said differently, Nick? Chloe asked after a while, the context lost to Nicole.

Who could possibly say? I don't even know where my phone is.

Chloe laughed and leaned in against Nicole, who had to lift her brush quickly to avoid a smudge. Ree had been watching and Nicole just noticed that she was being noticed and mouthed, *What the fuck, man?* to which Ree mouthed, *You know what the fuck, man*, but that proved to be too many syllables for Nicole to understand because lip-reading was not her thing, so she waited until Chloe was called to set before getting clarity.

What the fuck? she finally blurted like a sneeze she'd tried to hold back.

I had a dog, Ree said while capping his acrylics.

Nicole rolled her eyes, but she was enthralled. Oh Lord. Here is your wise magic Negro moment of the day.

Bitch.

Sorry! Continue, sir, lordship, Master Reginald.

My brother went off to the Navy when I was ten, so he let me have his dogs. They were named Taz and Eeyore.

Pooh!

What did I just say?

I'm sorry, she whispered.

Taz was a son of a bitch, never neutered, balls swinging, I-do-what-the-fuck-I-feel-like kind of motherfucker. I kid you not, bit everybody and everything in the neighborhood. The world was his. If it looked like something sweet, something salty, something soft, he had to bite it. He went to doggie jail, even, but the neighbors were illegal, excuse me, undocumented, so they didn't show up to press charges. Now, Eeyore, his brother, totally chill, had his cushion, had his water bowl, had his food bowl, and didn't bother anybody. But one day Taz was bored and said you know what, I want that cushion. So he started to chew and bite and tear every little bit of that cushion he could get to, even though Eeyore's fat butt was laying right on it. Then Taz went to Eeyore's water bowl and took a massive piss right in it. I kid you not. I'm getting to the point. Then Taz went for the food bowl. Eeyore leapt off the cushion, body-slammed into Taz, bit the hell out of him, and I was scared as fuck because I've never seen a big-ass lazy dog move like that. For the rest of their lives they kept that cycle up. Quiet, then rawrrrrr!

Nicole had a hand to her mouth.

What happened? she asked.

That's it!

What is the moral of the story? I am freaking out! What's the lesson?

If you don't know, you will never know.

Ree turned his back and put a piece of Juicy Fruit in his mouth. Nicole lowered her hand. She believed everything, though she would've preferred a metaphor where she did not have testicles, paws, and body fur. The temperament, however, matched perfectly. Peeing in water bowls was a young woman's sport. No more. Chloe was pretty and sweet and probably soft but firm where appropriate, and none of that mattered when bills and a job had to be done. Nicole had duties, most she forgot about and survived on luck and bright moments of undeniable talent, but not anymore. She would be professional.

Fourteen dolls each completed, singed and bloodied, the hardest part of the day done for the two of them. There was just the waiting, the touch-ups, the cleaning, the prep for tomorrow, and the thinking. A brilliant idea needed to come before 4:00 p.m. the next day when Dar would return to see the progress for the grand finale, Maximus Zombicus.

Nicole lived in a converted garage, permit free, in Santa Monica. The actual property belonged to parents of college friends who rented it out to the strange, hopeful, and financially liberal. LA is full of those special renters. When she returned home she unloaded her reusable shopping bags full of essential supplies and remembered her hunger, remembered her empty fridge, the decomposing tomatoes and red onions in jars at the back from her days of trying to pack salads for lunch only to become exhausted at the thought of packing a salad for lunch; two days of grilling chicken ahead of time, buying feta and dressing and arugula and layering it in folds like a beautiful English pudding was all she could manage before she was spending again. Seven dollars on coffee a day, and dollar-menu lunches when she was late to the craft service or there was no craft service or she needed to seem more conscientious and ate yogurt in public. Now the jars were science experiments with a colony of mold she thought fascinating because she made it happen and because there might be a cure for something in there. She remembered her phone and retrieved it from its long nap in the kitchen next to the Keurig: four messages, two from Ree, one from Dar, and one from her mother.

Aw shit, she said into her collar before listening to the message from her mother.

The voice was clear as water, each syllable exacting and pristine, full of hope and pride and love and biblical scriptures tinted with good old-fashioned condemnation and wonder and shame and declarations of the most obvious kind, which only made them that much more endearing.

Kiki, it is your mother. I am calling you now. You need a reminder as usual because I am sure you have forgotten about your new roommate. They are a drifting soul, as you know well. This is my pastor's sister's child, and you will be good.

I'm always good, Mama. I'm the good *one*, in fact!

Eight-ten in the morning, Kiki. You will forget if you do not set the alarm on your phone. That works for you.

What was she talking about?

Nicole replayed the message to get the parts she missed while talking to herself, the parts about picking up this stranger from Nassau at the airport at 8:10 a.m., which required that she not sleep if she was going to actually accomplish the task.

Shit, Mama.

After groaning into her refrigerator, Nicole did the most depressing thing she could think of: she ate gummy vitamins and a yogurt for dinner before sketching out another plan for the armor.

The delirium of wakefulness in spite of the need for sleep put a glaze over Nicole's eyes and mind and her perspective of what the world must see of her as she stepped around the LAX baggage claim. This was no ordinary pickup of a friend at the airport. Nicole was opening her world, her home, to an almost-stranger because they were a similar kind of strange, the kind that is abandoned, the kind that is often hidden and spectacularly frightening when suddenly made real. This was Nicole's great gesture of understanding and generosity to a fellow queer in need, which provided an opportunity to bond over their African American heritage, and as much as she desired to hold on to those noble intentions, there was another voice in her mind, dictating the scene back to her: her mother's.

Your body is eating itself, Kiki. You want to be skinny like the white girls, but you ate a large order of french fries and thirty-two chicken nuggets, and drank a venti mocha latte seventeen hours ago. Those are not good numbers. It does not add up. Waif. You want to be a waif. A waif is a wafer, a cookie. What is a cookie, Kiki? They are sweet and unhealthy and stupid. Do you want to be a cookie? There are barbecue packets about to explode under your car seats. Feel as beautiful as the Lord has made you. Cut your hair a little.

Nicole?

She jumped. The stranger jumped. The stranger gasped and jumped, actually.

Oh God. Joshua?

I'm sorry, so sorry.

No, it's fine, except I almost killed you!

The stranger laughed because Nicole was half his size, appeared intoxicated by most standards, and carried her world in a reusable shopping bag.

I go by Lorin, my middle name.

Okay, cool.

Nicole steadied her eyes and her heart to take in all of this new Lorin person, very tall to her, considering the height of everyone in Nicole's family peaked at five foot eight. Last they met, Lorin was Joshua, a young man who fifteen years ago Nicole recognized was a little too sassy and a little too smart for public adoration. He'd have a troubled life and here he was or she was or they were in artificial eyebrows and lip gloss. Lorin smiled to the left side and did not show any teeth, gray as the overcast morning in that bony sallow face, hair pulled back tight into a bun, shaved at the back, and wearing a tank top for a soccer club Nicole did not recognize, but she appreciated the gold accents.

Are you hungry? Nicole asked.

Starving, oh my God.

They shared a plate of novelty pancakes large enough to feed four people, but they were determined. She wanted to show off the soft sides of the city, the sweet balmy air and gritty dream-stained asphalt. Nicole learned that Lorin began transitioning from male to female three years ago at twenty-six, and Lorin was her grandfather's name; it worked because of the feminine sound, though was passed down from a Jewish businessman who gave the gene for finance to his son and blurry XY chromosomes to his grandson. Lorin was allowed to stay in a condo in the Bahamas that her father owned and never occupied. The hormones successfully atrophied her upper-body muscles, and Nicole could see the pride there from the way Lorin rubbed at her shoulders.

Wow. We should do a vacay! Nicole declared over a mouthful of pancake.

A kind of light slipped out of Lorin. The carbohydrate high dimmed at the mention of her former home, and Nicole knew not to mention it again.

I was never there much, Lorin said.

It took a few weeks for Nicole to realize just where Lorin must have been on that island when not at home. The dream of her new roommate did not quite match the stark full sensory reality. She learned just how small her garage conversion residence was with just the addition of a pair of men's size-twelve Nikes in the living room and the ladies' size-thirteen cheetah-print platforms under the kitchen table. Nicole dreaded the presence of a foreign body before going to the airport but secretly expected a hand-holding dervish the equivalent of chest-bumping basketball players coming together for a victory against the world that declared them outcasts, but Lorin seemed committed to doing other stuff whenever Nicole suggested they go to an improv show or eat at Umami Burger. Nicole realized that she did expect a friend from Lorin, and if not that, then a little bit of worship and admiration. Instead, a sharp ambivalence spilled out into her home and the two of them spoke very little and saw each other even less. Over those days she received the usual texts from Dar, always compliments, always a kind of sincerity that made Nicole nauseous. She still had one of Dar's T-shirts, old photos of them together that were nice enough to put in print. Their faces had no similar structure, so they made a terrible couple, except they were the same height. Dar had a shine to her like the light behind a closed door.

A bizarre kind of rejection and disappointment coated Nicole, and somehow that kind of emotional discontent becomes contagious, a willful contagion, Chloe the next infected. For a few days Nicole continued working with a little more reservation, but it was hard not to notice when Chloe was the one talking and Nicole was the one touching her affectionately. Chloe always seemed happy to sit down and mournful to leave for the set. It wasn't going to work, Nicole finally decided one day. When Chloe immediately sat in front of her to begin the day, Nicole moved away and passed her off to Ree. It was easy and cool, like stepping out of the wrong line at a bank, leaving the others in line to secretly wonder if they're in the wrong place too.

You're mine today, doll, Ree told Chloe tenderly.

He was sweet and Nicole was grateful and could not stand to look Chloe in the eye. Chloe tried to ask a question, but Ree was a better talker than all of them and swept her in another direction literally and figuratively. On the upside, Dar loved Nicole's plan, meaning she nodded dismissively, to incorporate a cluster of fingers and a hanging eyeball into the torso of Maximus Zombicus. She could breathe a little freer, her job security more stable. And other than feeling like she would throw up every time Dar put an arm around Chloe on set, things were looking up for Nicole until the felony incident.

She came home expecting it to be empty but slightly comforted by the thought that someone just might be there, just might be curious about her day, and felt safe because of the space she provided. These were big complicated feelings for seven o'clock in the evening and they slipped away slowly as the sun when faintly she heard a dog barking. She did not own a dog. Nicole entered and could hear the low raspy bark of a really large animal out on the shared patio, but more than anything she was met with a smell, a foreign smell, spicy as hummus but with a depth as inviting and repulsive as good cheese and baby powder. Then Nicole saw the source of this disorder, epithelial glands, lavender-based lotion, collarbone, hips, breasts, powerful forearms: a whole person. Lorin and what could be described only as a muscular Black transsexual woman in a long auburn wig and leather miniskirt stood in the kitchenette looking at Nicole, waiting, smiling. Behind them on the counter next to the kitchen sink were little plastic baggies folded neatly into each other, stuffed with an assortment of colorful pills. There were maybe twenty little baggies set out like tulip bulbs for the planting into hearts of men and women.

The auburn wig tilted above a wide smile, and a strong, heavily moisturized hand stretched out to Nicole.

I'm Marseilles Savage. Enchanté.

Nicole wanted to recoil and say, *No, no, no, you have this all wrong, the wrong house, the wrong day of the week, the wrong illegal substance, the wrong family. This is a house for cheap wine and fast food where fruit is bought ironically and thrift store shopping done out of necessity. There is only the rare and occasional marijuana use. You must go. All of this point in time must go.* Instead she offered her own hand to be gingerly swallowed by Marseilles's.

It's nice to meet you too.

I don't suppose you want a snack, Marseilles cooed while holding up a single white pill as if it were a banana or slice of bologna.

Lorin quickly pulled Nicole out of the house and into the backyard, leaving Marseilles alone in the kitchen.

What do you do when your brand-new trans roommate moves in and becomes a drug dealer? Panic. Remember the living arrangement, one of support and solidarity, two queers of color in a buddy comedy trying to survive the straight white world. Consider that this could be normal. Maybe this was normal, maybe it was a misunderstanding. Ask what is going on in a smooth nonplussed tone though inside both small and large intestines might release at any moment. Listen to a cell phone ring. Have hope for a resolution because there is an apologetic strain in your roommate's gelled eyebrows. Realize the apology is for the stranger on the phone. Remember soaking in a tiny bathtub with Dar, her body surrounding you like quicksand as she said how hard it must be for young straight women, the things they have to put up with. Decide to justifiably freak out. Grab head and chest and recall the organs necessary for life, will them into function. Recall the phone message from the landlord, that there will be a bid on rent, an auctioning of your home for eight years to which you would probably have the most laughable offer, meaning no offer. Resign to homelessness of sorts, the artist's destiny. Try to stop what could be stopped.

Nicole hurried back into the house.

You can't do that in here!

Nicole shouted but continued to be ignored by Marseilles. Lorin, still on the phone, seized Nicole by the elbow, but she spun in a circle to free herself while hyperventilating for a second or two. Man up, even, she thought, though as a lesbian feminist she remained aware of the sexist rhetoric that often dismisses the power of the feminine in exchange for more patriarchal ideals. Suddenly she appreciated the noncisgender women who had conquered her kitchen and felt an unexpected sense of awe and oppression all at once. Though outweighed by forty-eight pounds, she leaned in to the friend of Lorin's as she held Nicole's favorite cooking pot and said, "I will fight you!" And to that she received a smile and brief recognition of her humanity.

Hush, little goldfish.

Nicole exhaled and allowed herself to be led outside by Lorin for much-needed clean air and forgot about the previous sounds of a large foreign animal. She ignored Lorin's grip that was trying to keep her a little farther back and walked forward, arriving face-to-face with an enormous albino male American pit bull, magnificent, deadly. He possessed one blue eye and one gray. With little else left to do, Nicole dropped to the ground on her shins and waited to be mauled by Cerberus reincarnated, no will to resist. A tongue, soft and wet, fluttered on her cheek and then her palms as the animal cleansed the salt from Nicole's skin, tears and sweat. Lorin picked her up, muscles not as atrophied by hormones as they appeared. Placed her onto the wicker patio love seat as she looked Nicole in the eye and smiled, this time that apology really was for Nicole.

I made some friends, she said.

What else was there to do other than nod and laugh and cry and feel the exhaustion of the day all over again? Nicole felt silly and lost.

I made amazing ramen during the recession.

It was Lorin's turn to laugh and cry a little. The dog panted at their feet and for the first time Nicole felt the sense of family she'd been imagining and anticipating for so long.

But soon the voice came, the obvious, the echoes of a wiser woman with a better vocabulary and more exacting standards of behavior. Nicole said everything to Lorin that her mother would.

Your father is white and wealthy. Statistically, it is better to be white and wealthy when committing a crime. You are neither. Do you want to go to prison? Your friends are criminals, but they accept you. When they can afford to make you go away, they will. I can survive better in jail than you. They take everything from us there. At least

here you can be close to who you are. Dear heavenly father, thank you for the fact that it is not heroin. Amen.
We're sitting together now. Feel beautiful, Lorin.

Lorin did not reply, but it was still the longest conversation the two had had since the airport. After a few breaths
Lorin finally spoke, said people used to throw things at
her, rocks, cans, bullets out of guns while on the island.
She could've gone home where there was no one, but she
stayed out with her friends who were like her:

Magical.

Lorin smiled her gray smile, then hid it just as fast.
Nicole did not want to cry; she became angry, angry at
those forces she knew were there but had been partitioned
off from her life, that being more invisible than Lorin had
allowed her to do— And before she could continue her
rant someone opened the side gate to the yard, and Nicole
heard footsteps. She and Lorin looked to their right to see
a couple, white and cute and hetero as a pair of cotton
swabs, edging into the patio, their eyes scanning curiously
all around and finally landing on the bench.

We'll come back later, the presumed husband said.

They were too well coiffed to be dope fiends, so they
must've been potential renters though not confirmed. Nicole wasn't sure if it was the steely-eyed pit bull, the soft
butch lesbian, the transgender woman, or the overgrown
weeds that deterred the couple from approaching any farther, but she suddenly had the urge to go to a garden center and buy something purple in a pot.

The next day was supposed to be one of healing, nothing worse should've happened, if life was prone to fairness, an equal distribution of suffering and pleasure at all times, but life is prone to other things.

American lesbians are raging narcissists, Ree said over the brush between his teeth.

Yes, but can they legally do this?

Nicole referred to a letter she held from her landlord. The rent was going up and they were accepting bids.

Is that even a thing? she asked.

It sounds like a thing to me.

Then the set exploded. There were often loud noises in the studio, one can become accustomed to the usual indoor pyrotechnics, but to veterans of the industry a real life-threatening event is easy to distinguish. Ree and Nicole moved to each other and held arms for security while gazing at the ceiling so many stories away and waiting for the ground to stop vibrating. The two of them wandered out of their corner into the mayhem of dust and smoke. Dolls were screaming, gaffers cursed and clutched their gonads for a moment of clarity. Nicole looked around and saw two bodies on the floor and her heart caved. Then Chloe emerged from behind her holding a coconut donut in a bloody hand, her hair was torn off and neck skin peeling from fire exposure enough to reveal vertebrae. She was fine. She was also very young and very new to the world of special effects and thought this was part of the show.

Are you okay? Ree asked her, Nicole still stunned.

Chloe confirmed, then took a bite of donut, the white of the sugar and coconut flakes horrifying against the red of her blood-streaked arm and mouth. Eventually she understood, and tears welled when the emergency vehicles arrived, six people hurried off to the hospital.

We carpooled, Chloe said about one of the dolls who suffered a knee injury during the collapse of the set.

Nicole felt sorry for Dar even though her own prized finale prop that took forty-two hours of creation was destroyed in the explosion. There was a kind of freedom she had in not being Caesar, especially in moments like this with the republic slipping away so spectacularly.

I'll give you a ride, Nicole told Chloe, and drove her to a condo near Highland Park.

Chloe invited Nicole inside, her roommates all away on the great hunt for food, money, sex, and/or pills. The two of them went into the dark living room and Chloe began switching on lamps with barely any effort. Then she spoke and kept speaking as if everything she would've said in the time that Nicole forced them apart needed to be acknowledged. Chloe declared that she wasn't actually from Brisbane but a town a hundred miles from it; she thought Brisbane sounded like a place people would remember. Her mother called her every day, and she loved her. Chloe wasn't her real name either, but that didn't matter much. Nicole heard her own mother's voice suddenly from past slightly intoxicated evenings: Your father was a poet. He read William Carlos Williams to me in my ear, and we made love for days.

Let me help you get all that off, Nicole said about Chloe's makeup.

It seemed unnatural for them to be standing and facing each other or being side by side even. They went to the bathroom and Chloe sat on the toilet while Nicole removed her skullcap, which put them both at ease; this was their natural state, to sit and to stand, to touch and be touched.

Your hair is amazing, Chloe said as if she'd never seen it before. I feel like I know your hands better than I know your face.

Nicole could feel a sad story coming, rising up and out of Chloe from her sloped shoulders to burst from the crown of her head, and Nicole had an idea for the new rebirth of Maximus Zombicus, a way to fuse the myth of Athena born from her father Zeus's skull, but this would require a lot of fake brain matter. She was excited, then felt sad again for Chloe for whatever she would soon say.

I'm going to have the lead in *Mermaids from Space 2*.

The lead? That's great!

Then Nicole realized the cost of being a lead for Dar: the dating, the selfies, the public show that only occasionally became a vaginal show because there wasn't much press to be gleaned from actual sex. Dar was more concerned about the illusion of it and how fucking sexy that illusion would be with someone like Chloe at her side. Nicole thought how we sometimes make compromises, invite poison into our lives, and it can't be helped.

Oh, Nicole said with realization, and brushed the top of Chloe's head.

Chloe turned sharply at Nicole, her first angry face, and Nicole realized Chloe didn't deserve pity or anger. Nicole remembered the joke she'd made to Lorin when they first met, how she somewhat threatened to kill her roommate before she knew her name.

Don't think about it now, Nicole said to Chloe in a tone as mournful as possible, giving way to the space they were in and squeezing out any undue righteousness or pity. Now you get to let your tits out.

Chloe made a sound that must have been an Australian word for *what the hell*, then giggled tearfully.

I meant fins, let your fins out.

In a sudden leap of gratitude and tenderness, Chloe took Nicole's knee in one hand, her palm in the other, and kissed the space just above the wrist. Nicole was shocked and pleased and didn't know if she should make out with Chloe or knight her, but she understood the kind of guilt and joy that comes with being okay and safe when others aren't and what it means to act rather than let go, be doomed to fail and do it anyway. Dewitt, she thought. She thought about praying for herself, about Dar's clothes and how she always knew exactly where to find them, and about the accident and how it seemed like chance that she and Chloe were there together but it was intentional, inevitable. Just about all of the horror of the day had been scrubbed off. Chloe's skin looked raw but warm again with just a hint of the glue and paint like she'd fallen out of a gilded frame. Nicole rubbed at the leftover resin near Chloe's damp hairline that would not be moved and said at last after Chloe patiently endured being cleaned so carefully that it probably hurt a little, for some response to her kiss, to their future, if a compromise were even possible:

The rest will come off in the shower.

Young Woman Laughing into Her Salad

Time of Day: Sunset

Location: Santa Monica Pier

Product: Deodorant

Close-ups of two attractive women, youthful but not too youthful, as they stroll the boardwalk. Lights of the pier flicker to life in the fading sun. The day departs like a gown dragging across the ocean. Every frame is degraded, imitation thirty-five millimeter, grainy and tingly. The women have heavy eyelids from unnamed personal trauma or illicit substances and their sexiness peaks when they begin to jog to the entrance of an arcade. One is more cheerful than the other, shorter, wider, the accessory to the taller one, the true beauty, the girl next door, eerie in her fuckability, a siren, a sprite, a can with a dent in it. Their lips are full and slick, parted and waiting. It's warm, the shorter woman removes her letterman jacket, an ambiguous *V* on the chest pocket. Its leather sleeves contrasting with the heavy fabric of the rest, an enviable symbol of belonging. The true beauty mirrors the motion and removes her jacket, a floral blazer, as two young men join in as validators of being, as audience to their joy, confirming that it is real and remarkable. The women are bare-armed in tank tops knotted at the waist for a sliver of flesh above the waistline. They shoot tiny basketballs— missed and not missed. They play Skee-Ball. They fire at electric aliens. They jump in victory with arms to the sky, hug, and give flirtatious side-eye to their acquired men in the background. They throw cloth sacks at clown heads and toss rings around bottles. They break for snacks— corn dogs and salad, lifted to their face, invisible messes at the corners of their mouths that they wipe with a knuckle and laugh at jokes unheard, secrets not shared, and lean onto each other like sisters or lovers, wearing the young men like perfume in the air.

Time of Day: Noon

Location: Urban Boxing Gym

Product: Athletic Apparel

Black-and-white shots of feet jumping rope in worn sneakers, sweat on a racially ambiguous woman's neck, a mouth exhaling, boxing gloves, another mouth cringing in silent pain, two similar-looking women glaring at each other determined, dark eyed, slick. The taut ropes of the ring stretch and contract from unseen pressure. A glove hits a rib in sports bra. Another glove connects in slow motion to a cheek. The sound is thunderous. Water drips from everywhere and everything. The whole world is sweating and exhausted and then the two women collapse side by side on the wall of the gym. One offers to the other a bottle of water dressed in condensation. The drink changes hands like a promise and an apology. They lower their heads in laughter.

Time of Day: Night
Location: Dirty Motel
Product: Antidrug Propaganda

Two girls lay their heads next to each other, smiling up at the ceiling, giggling openmouthed. They are dirty and raccoon eyed with messy hair. Sounds of an amusement park echo around them as the pillow transforms into a blue sky. They are on a roller coaster. They are on a bed. They are on a roller coaster. They are on a bed. A male hand, monstrous and disembodied, presses into the grimy pillow near the head of the girl on the right. The pillows and their heads rock and jerk to a grotesque rhythm. Their hair lifts into the sky and falls back down onto a grimy pillow. The roller coaster comes to a stop and their smiles fade. A meth pipe appears from the male hand and they each inhale. We follow the hand along a dank motel room. It opens a door and a man is on the other side, headless, a new hand that enters while the other leaves and the door closes again. The new hand moves to the girls who lay on the bed. The hand grips the side of the pillow among faint blue vapors. The sky returns and the sounds of screams as the roller coaster begins again at full speed.

Time of Day: Early Morning
Location: A Screened-In Porch
Product: Yogurt

Two reasonably attractive young women, presumably sisters, sit on a bench swing and watch the morning unfold. Each dips a shiny spoon into a plastic cup. They exchange snappy banter about outsmarting calorie counts and having a vast range of fruit flavor options in a way that equates yogurt varieties to total personal autonomy and the freedom to do anything. Their history is pleasant and buried. All of the tension and fights and betrayals are forgotten because there is sweet dairy on their tongues and warm natural light around the space. A dog wags its tail from under the bench, a goldendoodle, bred for intelligent and eclectic citizens. Through smiles and a gentle manner, they sit shoulder to shoulder. The women are young but not gorgeous, no eye makeup or sleepy lids. Smart, overweight, carefree, fiscally conservative women should pay attention to these women based on the lighting, based on their friendly but not overly sexy attitudes. Each dips her shiny spoon into the cup again. After each dip they suck the spoon clean and softly moan in ecstasy.

Side Effects Include Dizziness, Ringing in the Ears, and Memory Loss

She forgets
the number of children she had and that she outlived them
    all
what pockets were for
where masturbation is appropriate
how to blink with both eyes
how hard to scratch an itch
her family
whole nations
how the dense pain of childbirth leaves the mind immediately,
    forever.
She forgets
the nature of ordinary people
that faces of strangers should not be surprising her the

way sea urchins or a horse suddenly urinating can be
surprising
what an itch is
wars
the lovely indescribable smell of clean women
space
the ocean
Jim Crow laws
how to avoid the cold: liquor
her childhood on a tobacco farm with parents who could
only afford free labor: her brothers and sisters
lighting fires between the tobacco rows to prevent frost
how to pluck her eyebrows into a fine arch
accidentally setting fire to the tobacco farm
her mother's tears in the moonlight as the fields burned and
the beautiful smell afterward
that she'd been in love just once and pretended twice.
She forgets
her favorite nephew, a color-blind old man who liked all the
same songs and sold pills without a prescription
Star Trek
two of her sons ate Vienna sausages until their hearts gave
out in consecutive years
only one of her children died happy
running away during the fire and losing two toes to frostbite
that three of her daughters loved men who were no good
the weight of men who know they've been lied to
dinosaurs
Canada and Ecuador

what it meant to use a toilet
how to get out of bed or write a to-do list
how to smile to a kind face
day comes before night and babies before menopause
her own name
solar panels
cattle prods
ginger beer
blood on her tongue from an overzealous fuck
fear of death
the Los Angeles riots
Anchorage
honor killings
Tupac and Biggie
black coffee with chocolate cake in the mornings
Christmas stockings
thrift store shopping out of necessity.
She forgets
how to swallow
her first dog and father died of kidney failure
her son-in-law with Epstein-Barr once mugged a pizza man
the absent toes make her limp like a wounded soldier
the smoky smell of familiar ghosts
there were people who loved her, who knew her in many
     hours with many faces on days
that have no record.

Difficult Subjects

I t all started when Winter Fairchild wanted to know what the *c*-word meant. We made a few guesses. Jackie Middleton said it was an ice-cream topping nobody liked. I mentioned frog genitals. Maria Luisa said a *c*-word is a lady who has no friends, which we thought couldn't be right. Ms. Merriweather overheard at some point like she always does and eventually made a big thing about it. We're still in the big thing. Ms. Merriweather was our fifth-grade teacher and was always thinking about school when nobody else wanted to. She wore dirty Chuck Taylors with turquoise buttons, my favorite color. When she sat down in her leather desk chair it always sighed like it was glad to have her back.

"Okay, all," began Ms. Merriweather. "I'm still waiting on curriculum approval, but we're going to start a new lesson series this month called Difficult Subjects."

We already knew this was coming. All of us had a lot of anxiety about sex and questions about, like, what is

anxiety anyway, and Winter Fairchild said we were going to talk about abortions sooner or later and to just get
used to it. Jackie started to cry, but on day one Ms. Merriweather just took a piece of chalk and slowly wrote on
the one remaining blackboard we roll out for nostalgia or
when Ms. Merriweather screams "no more screen time"
the words AMERICAN HISTORY. All of the classes were taking
on subjects Ms. Merriweather and the other teachers said
weren't in the textbooks the way they ought to be.

Winter Fairchild was disappointed about the lack of
abortion talk and I could tell she was going to be trouble.
Other than that the morning went on as usual, although
our free hour where most of us do some coloring or building forts with toys went on a little longer than usual. It felt
that way to me. Snack time didn't happen at all, which was
very strange. Eventually we all fell idle and bored and began distrusting each other more and more, when an "ambassador" from Mrs. Martinez's class came in carrying a
basket. I felt my stomach like a vacuum and hoped she
brought peanut-butter crackers. Instead the basket was
full of papers, neat and colored in crayons and markers.
The ambassador walked around and gave us each a piece
of paper with the same message. It read:

"Room A26 has a turkey. It is young and male."

We all began to whisper. Many gasped audibly. Winter
Fairchild flipped her amber ponytail in astonishment and
it hit me in the eye. We both looked to Ms. Merriweather
for confirmation.

"It's okay. It's okay," she said. "They are learning about propaganda."

She said the word slowly. I hoped she would write it on the board, but she only underlined our lesson. It did not take long before we dropped the papers and flung our toys again, scribbled in our books. I had no concept of turkeys, not to mention boy turkeys. I always thought of turkeys like sexless holiday gods; they were beyond me and inside of me like Christmas carols and Christmas ham. I forgot the turkey in the context of class almost instantly, especially when the snacks finally came. The day went on as usual, with math worksheets and a module on extinct animals of the Paleozoic period. There would be a spelling test in the morning.

At home my dad made Salisbury steak and asked me about my day. I told him it was a little confusing. He only smiled and nodded, then asked what was confusing. I knew that conversation. He always had an answer ready even if he didn't really, and sometimes that answer could turn into a lot of problems, like when my watch stopped working and instead of taking it back to the store he started ordering parts for it, one after another, one day after the next until the mention of a watch would make him angry and sweat. I never mentioned it and when fewer parts were delivered and the microwave stopped working he forgot about it, and I decided I would too and learned to look for the time through strangers or clocks on walls. He kept staring at me, waiting for me to tell him what was so confusing. I wanted to say snack time and maybe love and how Ms. Merriweather smells nice. Instead I said algebra. We were not studying algebra.

"Algebra already? That is a little advanced for elementary grades."

"Ms. Merriweather believes in us," I told him.

He didn't smile but nodded. I hoped something would break in the house that very moment and take his attention from me and Ms. Merriweather, but thankfully he didn't mention algebra anymore.

The next day went much like the previous. Lots of coloring, many growling stomachs, and then the "ambassador" returned from Mrs. Martinez's class. This time it was a boy I couldn't remember seeing before, faceless and bland, with a backpack unzipped and full of slips of paper. He moved with less grace than the previous ambassador and dropped the papers at each of our desks, some sliding off only to be caught quickly in the air. I read mine aloud:

"Room A26 loves their turkey and believes it is sacred."

Winter Fairchild crunched her slip of paper in her tangerine-sized fist and threw it. A few others did the same.

Ms. Merriweather immediately said, "Clean that up," and they reluctantly did.

Before that round of paper could be deposited in the trash, another ambassador came by. Two on the same day seemed incredible. This one had neat sheets of printer paper in a stack and left them on Ms. Merriweather's desk. Ms. Merriweather only glanced at the stack and left the room. Maria Luisa was the first to go to Ms. Merriweather's desk and take a look at the papers. Jackie screamed, "No, don't look," but Maria Luisa did it anyway. Winter got up and grabbed the top sheet. After that everyone hurried over to get a sheet. Maria Luisa had already memorized the message and recited it for those too far in the back to get a paper.

"They have named the turkey. It is Mr. Turkalupogus."

"Those idiots!" screamed Winter. "They don't even know what they have!"

By the time Ms. Merriweather got back to the room, half the stack of papers had been taken and a haphazard stack left in their wake. I tried to make the stack as neat as possible. She looked around unfazed, and the day continued.

Our usual idleness and hunger ceased during a brief interruption. Fourth-grade twins Brad and Heather Marshall came in the room silently and grabbed Ms. Merriweather by the crotch, then grunted like angry geese and departed. Ms. Merriweather just nodded and grimaced as if pulling an eyebrow hair, then turned back to us and said, "Toxic masculinity." The twins hurried back in as if they forgot something.

"It never happened," Brad said.

"You wanted it," Heather concluded, speaking to all of us before they both sauntered away, more slowly this time.

We felt something collectively, a kind of change we had no name for. Together we nodded. Jackie made a

squeaky sound with her breath. School had become fascinating now. Soon after, there came a time to deal with Mr.
Turkalupogus.

"We're meeting at the B stalls," I overheard Winter
whispering.

The B stalls were the second-floor bathroom that always
smelled like bleach and pee. Winter arranged a meeting
of the minds during lunch. I had to see what was going on.
Only half the class showed up, crowding into the three-
stall bathroom. Some standing gleefully on toilets and
others sitting awkwardly on the sinks. Winter waved her
hands to quiet everyone, and we all gazed expectantly
at her.

"That turkey is America," Winter said, "it is land and butter and money, and we are strong except for Jackie, and we
can have it."

"Yeahhhh!"

I didn't understand the comparisons, but Winter Fairchild always spoke with authority, like when she dismissed
the buttons on Ms. Merriweather's shoes as "political" and
no one knew what she meant, but we all believed it.

That night was a Wednesday. Dinner on Wednesday
was usually experimental. Dad gave up on the meal prep
of the week by then and created a hodgepodge of what-
evers: white rice with artichoke hearts and frozen salmon
fillets. It did not turn out well. He asked about school as
if he were apologizing for the meal. I told him it was like
nothing I had ever experienced. He laughed. I was encour-
aged, so I told him.

"We are learning about all the things that aren't in the textbooks." He didn't laugh, so I clarified as best I could. I told him what Ms. Merriweather said. "We're combating the revisionist sanitization of our nation's educational institutions."

I waited for the nod and smile, but he only let the half-chewed salmon sit on his tongue, mouth agape. He looked at me with his face torn between giggles, tears, or screaming, like when I asked if we could eat dinner by candlelight after I saw a commercial for a movie where the two actors looked like they loved each other and sat with tiny flames burning between them. He looked at me then like something suddenly went wrong and it might've been a little bit his fault. I knew I must've gotten it wrong. Ms. Merriweather spoke like a judge and a mom. I didn't know how to speak like either and couldn't bring that eloquence to my father when I wanted to most.

"What the hell is going on at that school?!"

He got on the phone, and I only felt ashamed and hoped no one would ask me to say anything again until I could practice speaking more like Ms. Merriweather.

At school the next day Jonah Green asked an important question of no one in particular.

"What's up with snack time?"

We were anticipating the delays in feeding. Jonah brought a family-sized bag of pretzels and started selling them under the table. I bought a handful myself.

The "ambassadors" came twice again but the first time

just dropped a stack of paper outside the door. No one waited, and all of us quickly hurried to the door.

"Ouch," said Jackie, being pushed out of the way.

The message read: "Mr. Turkalupogus is in training to do tricks, potentially lethal."

The next ambassador a few minutes later just threw the stack of papers in the room, letting the dozens of sheets fly like a curse.

"Mr. Turkalupogus is left unguarded, likely due to corruption," read Maria Luisa.

There were other flyers mixed in about a ferret and vanilla sandwich cookie three-strikes law, but we thought they were for Mrs. Okafor's class on the prison industrial complex, so we ignored them. Mr. Turkalupogus was everything.

"We go now!" Winter screamed.

Ms. Merriweather looked up from her breathy leather chair and novel, eyes wide and unchallenging, while Winter led us out of A12 down the hall to A26. The heavy door burst open under Winter's tangerine fists. There he was, Mr. Turkalupogus, in a cute little pen. He did not have the majesty of a fully grown turkey. He was gray and svelte and big-eyed. Winter lunged for the turkey, and I could see her planning and not knowing exactly what to do but knowing that whatever outcome would be glorious and the only inevitable thing. Winter seized Mr. Turkalupogus by the total body, smashing his wings to his frame, shooting his neck rod-straight in terror.

"Don't do it!" and "Yeahhhhh!" were the only audible human sounds before a snatching tear struck the room.

The change happened again. Winter pulled the wings separate and tore Mr. Turkalupogus into two pieces across her chest like a wrestler splitting his T-shirt for applause. In the wreckage, others dived for the scratching flailing creature's remains and a couple put his feet between their teeth and bared down on the bones. Their own molars found surprisingly little resistance. I wanted to stop them but could only look at my hands.

Phalanges, I thought, metatarsals. Two hundred and six bones in the adult human body, more in infants, for some strange reason, a quiz next Thursday, 37.2 trillion cells make up a single person, all talking to each other about a scratchy throat, itchy scalp, the cycle of hunger, comedones forming in the epidermis, cancerous uprisings in the lower intestine to be thwarted, and increasingly rapid heartbeat due to unthinkable causes. I imagined my distal, middle, and proximal phalanges sucked into Winter Fairchild's mouth in retaliation for not participating, for quiet condemnation, and I looked to Ms. Merriweather (now in the doorway); the plea in my eyes did not go un-recognized. She said my name as if expecting me to fin-ish her own sentence, to cast some final judgment on the great mess at hand.

Because I said nothing, she looked at Winter, still writhing gleefully in the feathers and bird blood. Noth-ing coherent would come from her until the ecstasy of violence dissipated, so Ms. Merriweather turned to Maria Luisa, who was already brushing fluff from her sweater and straightening her shorts.

"Maria Luisa, what does Mr. Turkalupogus symbolize?"

Maria thought for a moment and said, "Vegans."

There was a silence, then some ohhhhs and other shouts in protest over the quieting sobs of Mr. Matsumoto's class, the original occupants of room A26, as they huddled together for comfort and protection.

"It's the planet!"

"Dinosaurs!"

"Black people!"

"Islam!"

"Indians!"

"Factory farming!"

"Jesus!"

"The sun!"

"The rain forest!"

Ms. Merriweather sucked her teeth, shook her head, and sighed. She looked in my direction again, and this time so did everybody. The room smelled like a billion dirty pennies.

"What does it symbolize?" she asked again.

"Me," I said in a whisper.

A few laughed, and then stopped.

"All of us," Maria said coolly, still plucking the infinite bird fluff from her sweater.

"Nice work," said Ms. Merriweather. "Tomorrow we will cover nuclear holocaust."

I mouthed the words after her. We all headed back to our classroom to finish the day, but there came a banging sound from the halls toward the entrance of the school. I could see my dad through the thick glass, sweating and angry. There were dozens of them, all the parents pounding the doors of the school, waiting for the guards to unlock them. The end of the day was near. Ms. Merriweather did not look away from the shouting mothers and fathers. I wanted to tell her no, to go the other way, to find her sensibly priced fuel-efficient vehicle in the parking lot via a different route and escape into the night and never come back to this place, but she ignored my wordless expression and moved on beyond the guards, unlatching the doors, and into the parents with their teeth bared and hands stretched out for her.

Trial of Ghosts

Rowina often pretended monsters were chasing her while riding her bicycle to keep her pace effective for fat burn. She did that as a child for fun, now for other reasons. She ran from grief. Monsters were no longer hideous grisly ghouls. They were echoes of people she'd known, returned to her for their own purpose. Rowina grew up watching TV shows about the dead like everyone else. One episode was about a soccer coach who lost her whole team in a plane crash. Every single one of the players returned to her. They didn't go to their own mothers and fathers or pastors or friends. They went to her, one at a time, for a month and nine days. The audience audibly awed at the love they saw from those dead children, but the coach looked like she hadn't slept well since and never would again. Another episode featured a confused man who had never been visited by anyone and didn't understand why, so he eventually developed a ghost fetish. He was not at all a mystery.

There were the bestselling books: *Are Your Dead Keeping Secret Bank Accounts?*; *How to Get the Dead to Do Their*

Chores; *Sexing the Spirits*; and *I Ain't Afraid of No People*, a memoir from the deceased.

Rowina ran from all of it. Though she was riding on the cement path winding along Ocean Drive, it was hot for early afternoon, too hot. She pumped her pedals relentlessly despite the heavy warmth, tiny rivers of sweat running along her throat and arms. A man in khaki dress pants and a white tank top, with dark hard slender muscles and a silk tie knotted loosely around his neck, kissed the air as she passed him.

"Slow down, baby girl!" he shouted.

The man looked like someone plucked from another country and dropped into the city like a doll. Women with carts for stowing groceries or laundry scattered the sidewalks along with couples and tourists. Teens rode scooters recklessly for as long as their dollars could power them, then cast them aside like trash to clog the path. Usually a speedy pace kept cool air rushing over her skin while she avoided the obstacles of the city, but not today. Today she raced through a veil, the air thickening as she lost energy. Rowina pushed herself too far again, and didn't want to pass out in the street with her bicycle pinned under her like a dead horse. That would be embarrassing. The water bottle wedged on the frame of her bike turned out to be of no help, a few warm beads of liquid were all that lingered inside. Her vision darkened around the edges, little spots formed ahead of her, and she knew she had to stop for hydration.

She'd been riding for over an hour and made it all the way into Seal Beach. Small yachts and catamarans jostled each other in the marina like friends. Fewer and fewer people appeared, and Rowina felt some relief because of the absence of bodies. She knew a place to go, a small café she didn't venture to too often, only when she needed a small escape from her fellow man and felt the excessive bill would be worth the price.

Though underdressed in black bike shorts and a white T-shirt that clung to her, she entered with only a little hesitation upon seeing her own reflection in the glass door. Her brown arms were firm and shoulders squared and solid from her weight-lifting routine. A toned long body paired with her soft full features searing with life and color from exertion gave her nothing to be displeased about. Plus, with a bike worth as much as a used car chained out front, the staff would know she could afford the check.

Once she was through the door the air conditioner restored her faith in this world. She held up a single finger to the host without smiling to indicate how many would be dining and was escorted to a seat immediately. The café was just as she expected, nearly empty on a Saturday during peak lunch hours. An attractive waitress appeared wearing a black apron down to her ankles and blue button-up shirt tucked into her waistband.

"Would you like to start with some water?"

Rowina looked up and nodded with feigned desperation that earned her a small smile in return. The waitress returned with water and a basket of bread with a saucer of olive oil and seasoning.

"I'll give you a minute to decide, hon."

Rowina was finally alone to drink and drink and drink after pulling the unsolicited lemon from the glass. When the water was more than half gone, she had the where-withal to notice she was not as alone as she thought.

A woman sat facing Rowina only two tables away and stared directly at her. Rowina couldn't be sure how long the woman had been staring or for what reason. After a brief panic, Rowina looked away, as is customary when making accidental eye contact. She looked back to make sure the woman too had looked away, but no, she stared on. The panic returned hotter than ever. What did she see? Rowina couldn't help but rub a hand along the back of her head, having just cut her hair short around the sides for the first time since college. She glanced down at her shirt, which had been drying well, no sweat stains. Then she checked her own reflection quickly in the window. From what she could see, nothing seemed out of the or-dinary. Another wave of panic hit, as if the woman could see into Rowina's wallet and accounts and see every late payment and overdue bill and was judging her unworthy, a fraud and a fool. But that was impossible. There was no evidence on the surface to indicate anything problematic unless the woman was a racist or a psychopath. In that case, Rowina decided to stare back. The woman didn't wa-ver at all under the new scrutiny. Rowina saw her strapless dress and lightly tanned skin, dark eyes and hair that fell in

gentle coils past her shoulders. She would've been beautiful if she weren't so invasive, Rowina thought. A motion
near the kitchen distracted Rowina's gaze just enough to
see the staff fumbling with an order. When she returned
to the woman she was gone, or so Rowina thought before
realizing the woman was on her feet and walking toward
Rowina's table.

Well, this was it, whatever it was Rowina couldn't be
sure, but she mentally prepared herself for the worst, a physical assault perhaps, a verbal scolding. Maybe the woman
mistook her for a mistress and planned to have it out.
Rowina smiled briefly at the thought of being yanked on
and cursed at by a beautiful woman in the name of a forget-
table husband. She might let it go on longer than necessary.
The two could laugh about it and maybe Rowina would
get an apology meal out of the whole ordeal. That thought
didn't last long when Rowina detected subtle nerves in the
woman, how she pressed her palms against her thighs to
smooth wrinkles that weren't there or wipe away anxiety
moisture. What did she have to be worried about? That
made Rowina worry even more. Was that what women
did before they reached into a designer handbag and pulled
out a gun to kill their partner's lover? Was that what they
did when they wanted to know the time? Rowina thought
she had women figured out but now wondered if she knew
women at all. Then it was too late because the woman
stood over Rowina, and the moment had arrived for the
end of her life or something short of it.

"Excuse me, but I think I know you," the woman said.

She smelled of vanilla, and Rowina lost the edges of the room for a second. There was no anger in that voice, just low soothing notes of uncertainty and something else, maybe hope.

Rowina shook her head and her hand returned to the back of her neck when the woman laughed unexpectedly and profoundly. It was an unmistakable laugh, familiar in its absurdity, like a tiny sprite gasping for dear life. Rowina knew that laugh like she knew a stone dropped in water.

"Mani?"

"I haven't heard that name in years. I became the whole Amani to everyone in the end."

She glanced at the chair across from Rowina for permission to sit. Rowina nodded and leaned forward on her elbows, astonished. There she stood. Perfect.

"You look . . . so . . . I didn't recognize you until the laugh. There it is."

Amani took a deep breath to quiet the giggles. The waitress returned with Amani's place setting and water glass.

"Can I get you two any appetizers?"

Rowina already shook her head no in response to the unnecessary, exorbitantly priced, and inadequately portioned "appetizers" the café probably had to offer, while Amani replied in the affirmative.

"Definitely. Let's start with the salmon rolls? Right, Ro? And the mixed greens. The tuna tartare is pretty good. We can share all that."

"Sure."

Rowina stared at the menu, eyes flitting from one price to another so quickly from the spike of adrenaline that she didn't see the waitress disappear. When she looked up she found Amani staring at her intently. She could feel the slump in her back, so she straightened immediately. She had a balance on one credit card to cover the sum so far, but might have to run the risk of a declined transaction if the orders progressed any further. Amani couldn't know any of that, especially if she sat upright and kept her eyes focused on the present and not the past. But what did the dead know? How far could she reach into her soul, her mind? Rowina shook her head. She was being silly. They don't come back for that, to know things about us and shame us with private information. Amani of all people would never know any of that if Rowina held herself together. She could just say no. When the food arrives, I'll say no thank you, she thought. She could say she'd had a seafood aversion lately. That would be convincing. Rowina considered all of this with Amani's dark eyes leveled on her as if she could pull the thoughts out and lay them on the table like a deck of cards.

"It's good to see you, Ro. It's been forever."

"It has. I . . . I . . . you've been gone awhile."

"I've been gone?"

That laugh again.

"Where did I go? I never left the state before the end. You! You went everywhere."

Rowina smiled. This wouldn't be so bad, this visit. She could handle this just fine, not like the other, her mother's visit.

"I did some traveling. Lived abroad for a stint on different fellowships."

Amani nodded and sipped her water. Then ran her fingers along the condensation.

"You were the smart one," Amani said, not looking up from the table.

Her voice became low, pensive and weighty. Rowina traveled after graduate school to residencies. Eventually the fellowships ran out, but the wanderlust remained, fueling a wildfire of debt she had yet to extinguish.

"I know who you married, at least," Rowina said. "Everyone knows who you married."

Rowina laughed, expecting to hear that thrilling chuckle from Amani, but no sound emerged.

"Not everyone."

"Please. The waitress knows who you married, Mani. Even if they don't know you."

The last of those words moved Amani back in her chair a little. Rowina didn't mean to sound hurtful, but she had hurt Amani. The way her cheeks drew in and her bottom lip shifted from side to side, almost comical, like a baseball player about to spit, but here she was, a woman who once had everything, mildly offended because she wasn't as famous as her spouse. Well, Rowina knew better than that. When Amani was hurt, it was better to duck out of the way of whatever she did next.

Crying was the least of anyone's worries. Rowina would know, having been the cause of some pain she hadn't thought about in years.

Amani had lived abroad until age eight, when she arrived at Rowina's elementary school. Her father was French and met her mother in a central African country while on service duty. When her mother died of a degenerative disease, Amani traveled alone with her father. She showed up in Rowina's class with the wrong accent, the wrong hairstyle, the wrong parent. Rowina knew what it was like to have a dead mother and how well-intentioned fathers sometimes didn't think through an outfit carefully. Amani fit in just right with Rowina. In grade school they were inseparable. When two smart girls with imaginations cling to each other, only fools try to pull them apart. Together they pretended to be lions and hunters, taking turns at being prey or predator, gnawing at each other's limbs and judging the flavor. "Sweet. This lion must eat a lot of cereal," or "This one is no good, too much broccoli." Their games evolved as they pretended to be each other's mother, seeing as they both had none. Clumsily offering care to one another as any imaginary mother would, spooning soda into each other's mouths as medicine or baking beautiful birthday cakes made of air and dreams. Eventually they pretended to be each other's sister, then wife or husband. Rowina put a hand on her hip and scolded Amani for not appreciating all her hard work, maintaining their invisible home and taking care of their stuffed-animal babies. Amani would take fake sips from a brown bottle stolen from the trash, then laugh and laugh, then hug Rowina tightly in mock apology. Then the roles would switch. Rowina would get to be a lazy husband and Amani the overworked wife.

Not long after that, Rowina's own mother visited her.

It took her too long. Her mother waited wherever the dead wait. Rowina had forgotten her, forgotten her eyelashes and chin hairs and smell of astringent and lotion. Her long fingers and braided hair, none of it seemed like a part of Rowina. They were fragments that belonged in photographs. Rowina had a mouthful of pancake when her mother entered from the backyard kicking her sandals off by the door. Rowina screamed. Her father came running out of the bathroom. Once he realized his dead wife had come to see Rowina and not him, he had to leave. "It'll be fine, Roro. I'll be back soon."

He left. He left her with a dead woman rummaging through the kitchen for a spoon to stir sugar into some coffee.

Rowina screamed at the door, more angry than terrified at being abandoned, but when the scream broke away from overuse, they were still there together.

A month later, Rowina invented the witching game for her and Amani to play at school. They sat together on the blue and yellow reading carpet, tearing construction paper into tiny pieces and throwing them into a circle for spells to make them grown-ups or airplanes, anything that could fly away. A loud girl with a pink spring-loaded umbrella pulled at Amani's shoulder, then aimed the umbrella and hit Amani in the cheek just under her eye socket. The girl bent over in laughter as Amani's tears started immediately. Rowina didn't have a chance to react before Amani leapt into the air and snatched at the girl's head, scratching deeply and yanking that stupid umbrella away and bashing her until the teacher came and lifted Amani up like a melon, a wailing melon with a fistful of another child's hair and tears and mucus running down its face. While hovering under the teacher's arm, Amani saw Rowina with her little hand deep in the pile of torn paper, then she stopped wailing. Their eyes met, wide and curious, believing they had made the moment happen.

As they got older, the boys tugged, but it wasn't until the boys had something more substantial to offer than their bodies that Amani bothered to look up.

The waitress brought the appetizers, enough for five people by Rowina's estimation. Amani wasn't as famous as her husband, but their fame didn't really matter at all in Rowina's circles. She did know it mattered to Amani, and that was all that counted. As a gesture of goodwill and apology, Rowina reached for a salmon roll instead of refusing the plates altogether as she'd planned. She would pay this small price this one time.

"Did you save the world yet?" Amani asked, not eating, just watching Rowina.

That was confirmation enough that Amani had something on her mind, and Rowina wasn't going to leave that café without having those thoughts come down like boulders.

"Mani, what's your problem?"

"What are you talking about? I was just curious. Your accounts are private, or they were last I checked, so I was wondering what you were up to."

"Oh. You're in love with me."

"Shut up!"

Amani choked a little on her water and laughed as Rowina had intended.

"You're the same, you know that?" Amani continued.

"Smart, hot, super cool?"

"And kind of an asshole."

"I heard *and*, so I won't argue with any of that."

Rowina's phone alerted, but she silenced it without looking as Amani began to eat. So, all the dead can eat. Rowina was thankful for that, otherwise she might be obligated to pay for all of the appetizers. Another question more urgent than the last surfaced. Rowina opened her mouth to speak but quickly denied herself.

"You can ask me anything. That's sort of why I'm here."

"Are your credit cards working?"

Amani smiled and nodded.

"Everything works. Cards. Cash. Heart. Lungs."

"So, what's it like?" Rowina asked.

"What?"

"Money!"

"Oh! It's never as much as you expect, I guess."

"That sounds right."

The waitress returned ready to take the full order, but Rowina leaned away from her as if asked to participate in a medical experiment.

"I probably have plenty, and it's getting a little late."

Amani slid her hand across the table as if to reach for Rowina but came just short of actually taking her hand.

"We can finish lunch, can't we?"

The words were too sincere for Rowina to bear. She would agree to anything when Amani spoke like that, as if there were no other people in the room, as if begging weren't beneath either of them when it came to each other. Rowina could only nod and eye the menu, still lurking on the edge of the table, with suspicion and scorn.

"Club sandwich for me," Amani said with such a confident shift in timbre that Rowina thought she'd been duped.

"Same."

The waitress smiled, scooped up their menus, and left them alone again. Amani looked at Rowina, not saying anything, eyelids low and a smirk on the edge of exploding as if she'd won something. Rowina's skin had cooled too much in the air-conditioning; now she felt underdressed as goose bumps rose on her forearms.

"No, I haven't, by the way," Rowina said. "The world still needs saving."

"I'm sure. Who are the villains now, other than me and the whores of capitalism?"

"Ha ha ha," Rowina deadpanned.

"Seriously, Rowina. There's a crisis for someone every day. I worry about you, you know."

"Me? We've got widespread domestic terrorism, government complicity and abuse, income inequality like never seen in the history of mankind, and you know what happens to people who say something about it? Dead. We're in a fucking dark age, a war, and you're worried about me?"

"Yes, you! I didn't know about the protesters, but it is okay. It's okay, you know, to have someone worry about you."

Amani spoke to Rowina as if she were aware of her tendency toward theatrics, as if Rowina's proclamations were well rehearsed, performed, and a proper audience reaction was all she really wanted. Rowina considered all of the reactions she should've gotten, the ones she was ready for, the denials, the apathy, the smug disregard for class distinctions, for a safer retort about all people being spiritual beings because it is necessary for the privileged to not worry about the safety of the disadvantaged, which makes the privileged think they're safe when they rightly suspect otherwise. Rowina knew what to say to those people, the ones who wanted to live above the trees where screams are buried in the wind. Coward. Blind. Weak. Selfish. Amani, however, was none of those.

As children, they were different but similar. Rowina was being raised by a single father, but she had aunties aplenty. She went to school washed and styled and ironed. Among the poor kids she looked pristine. Among the rich kids she looked loved. When Amani showed up to elementary school, motherless, her hair a frizzy cloud, and towing a backpack on wheels, she was teased mercilessly for half a day, no evidence of love to protect her. During the second snack time, a boy pulled her hair hard enough to draw a tear. She squeezed a pack of peanut-butter crackers in her fist and told him in French to eat a dead man's foot. The boy stopped as if his throat had been slit. She said it again, a flurry of vowels and consonants, another cut. She said it again faster, and another wound opened in his heart. The boy wailed like he'd been cursed. Rowina was in awe. The teacher came over to Amani, who stood quietly, innocently, nearly crying too, and maybe to the teacher her wet eyes shone like empathy instead of condemnation. The teacher took the boy out to the restroom to calm him down. Rowina immediately sat next to Amani without saying anything at all and could feel the heat of anger still rising from her little arms. The two of them opened their crackers and began to eat. She wasn't teased again, at least not by that class. Years later, Rowina asked what was said to that boy, and Amani confessed she'd never heard anyone say eat a dead man's foot before or after that day; the words just came out of her. The two of them laughed and laughed.

"I'm surprised you're not married," Amani continued at the café. "Are you close, perhaps?"

"Are you flirting with me, Mani?"

Rowina leaned forward and Amani's involuntary intake of breath betrayed the truth.

"You never did play fair," Amani replied, suddenly fascinated with the texture of her napkin.

"I always played as if I could win."

In high school Rowina convinced Amani to join the track team. No one teased the athletes, but by then everyone's personal trauma became so cumbersome that bullying had gone out of fashion anyway. The two of them kept up their games, though, of prey and predator, of mother and daughter, lover and fool. They didn't always want to play at the same time. One afternoon on the track field, Rowina had bad cramps and Amani felt a joy and lightness inside that almost made her want to kill someone. They lined up in the lanes. Amani sensed Rowina's nausea, then swatted at her for being vulnerable. When a predator spots a victim there's little that can dissuade it from attack. Amani ran side by side with Rowina, still playfully swatting at her when Amani was sure the coach couldn't see. Rowina yelled at her to stop it. Amani bared her teeth and growled with a smile. Somehow turning to each other full-on ruined the trajectory and their feet tangled in a devastating fall. They rolled over on each other before coming to a stop, bloody elbows and foreheads well-earned.

"Aw shit!" the coach yelled.

The two of them went to the lockers for first aid after receiving a few more chastising swears from the coach, Rowina too angry to even speak. She went into the cage with all of the equipment, opened and slammed the cabinets looking for something remotely first aid in nature, then kicked a sack of soccer balls that spilled out on her foot. Amani stood quietly by the door to the cage, holding her elbow. Only when Rowina finally found the case of rubbing alcohol and bandages did she look at Amani and see just how much damage had been done. Amani took the brunt of the tumble. Rowina had what might be a bad bruise on her hip and shoulder but no blood on her face.

"See what you did?" Rowina said. "If you'd listened to me the first time, we wouldn't be here. Kids never listen."

"I'm sorry, Mommy."

"Sit over here, you little dumbass."

Rowina gestured for Amani to go to the benches near the lockers. The first-aid kit exploded when opened, bandages fell to the floor in a hurry. After a skeptical look at the messy contents, Rowina made a selection: an alcohol wipe, some ointment, tape, and a few cotton pads. Once the blood was cleaned and Amani patched up she growled again, the urge to kill not quite satiated.

"Shut up," Rowina said, looking her in the eye.

Amani growled lower, and this time Rowina growled back. Amani lunged at Rowina and put a soft bite on her cheek. Rowina screamed in shock and delight, falling off-balance, and knocked the first-aid kit to the floor. Amani crawled on top of Rowina and made an exaggerated sniffing motion around Rowina's face and neck, stopping when their eyes were level. Rowina smiled and gently bit Amani on the chin, a slow acceptance of her bizarre apology. Amani's hands loosened their animal grip on Rowina's waist and shirt. They looked at each other, closer and for longer than they ever had before. All the clichés are true about how love strikes at the heart, how it rings like a bell in the chest and reverberates throughout the spine. Amani kissed Rowina. Her chapped lips mashed against Rowina's mouth, growing warmer and wetter and more suffocating by the second. They didn't kiss as hunter and prey or as if in friendly game. They kissed like lovers recognizing each other for the first time. After a few minutes, they were calm again and sat in silence. Eventually Rowina stood and Amani followed. They scavenged some expired ibuprofen from their coach's desk drawer and went back to the field.

The two got older, taller, stronger. Time changed their shape and altered how everyone, especially men, perceived them. The boys became their own dense units patrolling the school and streets. Amani didn't see them until the athletic scouts came to town. Women's sports didn't come with the potential of new cars and exposure to professional opportunities. The men's sports did. Before that time, it was enough that Amani and Rowina paid attention to each other, but a foreign promise emerged: money. When a senior with a new Mustang gifted by some university in Texas asked Amani on a date, she immediately sought Rowina's advice, and, in a way, permission. It was exciting for both of them, to be wanted by someone of value to the world at large. Things were fine after the first couple of dates. Amani recapped unenthusiastically before falling asleep on the couch with her hand under Rowina's shirt. With each new encounter Amani became more fascinated with the workings of athletic scholarships and how much a contract could be worth if the trajectory toward professional status, merchandising, and endorsements continued. One evening, they had a pot of spaghetti waiting for them as dinner courtesy of Rowina's father.

"Are you staying tonight?" he asked Amani while halfway out the door for his graveyard shift. Amani was in mid-nod when Rowina replied for her.

"Not tonight."

Amani turned as if she'd been kicked. The door closed. They looked at each other for a long time. Rowina didn't have the words for jealousy and didn't know that it was possible inside of herself until then. She could only punish them both for it. They would sleep cold and apart that night and many more to come.

"Remember how your dad was always mad at something nobody ever thought about?" asked Amani, one hand over the other on the café table.

"Vaguely," Rowina replied, disingenuously laughing a little, giving herself away.

"C'mon! The recycling bins!"

Rowina laughed. "I haven't thought of that in years."

"He was all, why they gotta be a different color? Trash is trash. They should all just be clear, then nobody gotta be worried about a code." Amani mocked in a gruff man's voice.

"He got that citation from the city for putting yard waste in recycling."

"Is that what it was?"

"That and horoscopes."

"Oh my god, the horoscopes! How they gon' know what happened on my birthday a thousand years ago when everything in the sky is dead anyway? Starlight is billions of years old, those stars have long blown up. They don't even count!"

Laughing, Rowina held up a hand to stop Amani from continuing.

"I don't know how he could be the sweetest man and harbor so much hate for recycling bins. He did have a point about the stars," Amani said.

"Did he? Sure, the body is gone, but the light is still there, the energy maybe. All the lights in the sky are just ghosts, tugging on us, this way or that. If we have to be pulled by something dead, why not starlight?"

Amani became very still and put her hands in her lap. She didn't laugh anymore.

"How is your dad, Ro?"

Rowina smiled and shook her head. Amani sighed.

"When?" Amani was almost angry in response.

"A year ago almost."

The waitress brought their meals in the silence between the two. Plates slid against the wood, one after another.

"Enjoy."

"Thank you," the pair said in soft unison.

"Has he come to see you?"

"Not yet. No. No, he hasn't."

"My dad never came to see me either. I used to feel angry about it, you know? Like who did he choose anyway? Some hooker I never met?"

"Maybe." Rowina smiled. "So you stopped being angry about it. We weren't chosen. We weren't enough to come back for."

"But that's just it, isn't it, Ro? We were enough. We lived together with those men and never had anything left to say. It was complete, a day started, a day finished. Release between the dead and the living has to be mutual. Your father loved you, Ro, and never had anything else to say about it."

Rowina could taste the bitter aioli and feel the muscles in her neck and shoulders seize upward, the ache behind her eyes.

"We're almost out of time, Ro."

Amani smiled at her. That seemed the worst point of the day to Rowina. The mention of time struck her like a cramp. She had questions. Why did you choose

me and no one else? Can it be undone? Is death temporary? But she knew all of those answers from seeing her
own mother before she left the second and last time.
They don't come back again, and you don't get more
time. Amani sat quiet, smiling, her skin flushed, every
freckle vivid. Her lips separated, on the verge of speaking, then abandoned the impulse. Instead she stared at
Rowina, waiting. The memory of Amani continued to
pulse, warm and suffocating. The dead come back to listen, Rowina remembered from somewhere. You can say
anything to a ghost. It's supposed to be liberating, en-
lightening, freeing, a final judgment of things unsaid,
but to be alive just then seemed laborious and unbearable and something else, like victory or avarice. She
didn't hate Amani or pity her or herself or even mourn
her as she should have, but if there were words for kicking a woman while she was down on the ground, Rowina wanted to say them, to gloat for having hot blood
and breath and the sun on her arms, for Amani being
so reckless in love and calculating in everything else.
Why couldn't that be reversed just once in her brief life
and maybe everything would be different? Maybe they
would've loved unabashedly until old age, unrecognizable to the past, doing gentle yoga classes together
every other day, making love with bodies only youths
find terrifying, walking through museums with docent
fierceness, reveling in that marvelous surprise of finding
another person standing beside you who is yours.

When Rowina's dead mother made herself a plate of eggs and sausage before taking a seat at the table, Rowina continued to scream as the eggs were eaten one forkful at a time, the coffee drained and meat consumed. When only hoarse rasps remained in Rowina's throat, her mother spoke.

"Is that all you have to say to me, then? Aren't you worried about becoming a woman?"

Rowina closed her mouth and thought of herself as a thing transforming, changing like some cartoon insect on a video during science class, except in the videos the narrator never asks the bug if it's worried. She and Amani had played at being mothers, imagined them religiously, all their mannerisms and funny words. The mothers they played were perfect because they were there inside of them to call forth whenever the moment demanded. Rowina hadn't been worried about becoming a whole woman on the outside unable to retreat back into the body of a child ever again until then, and her mother seemed satisfied with that. As if to worry was the real lesson, the only lesson worth knowing as a girl. Her mother got up and washed and dried her plate before returning it to the cabinet. She hung the towel on the stove handle after shaking it straight, then headed to the back door, slipping on her sandals and leaving without turning around.

At the café, Rowina felt stupid, an ordinary kind of stupid for having wasted so much time in her own mind hating someone she loved because she was afraid of losing that love to begin with.

"You are the worst of all, Mani," Rowina finally said. "Of all my dead. This is the worst."

Amani laughed and took Rowina's hand, nails indenting her skin, pressing deeply, unyielding, wanting to get closer than ever possible as always.

Part II

Grief Log

EXERCISE	SETS	WEIGHT	REPS	GOALS	EXECUTION	JUSTIFY
funeral for Daddy	three locations: church, grave, house	whatever two whole buildings, thirteen cars, a limousine, seventy people, six babies, and all their reasons weigh	one circle around the casket, one circle around the cemetery, one circle around the backyard, nine circles from the kitchen to the living room	cry, feel better	Mama doesn't cry, everything hurts, everything splits open	love doesn't look like that for us

EXERCISE	SETS	WEIGHT	REPS	GOALS	EXECUTION	JUSTIFY
aunties visit	eight hugs	563 pounds of women	stand there and take it arms to the side	feel better	feel better	the aunties smell like lavender and bacon
Pastor Short visits	one hug	an elephant seal with a #7 haircut, looking at a thing no one really believes in	once is enough	get him out	feel like throwing up	he tells me and T we're pretty like our mother
house empties	the door opens and closes eleven times	nothing, just ghosts alive and not	eight pairs of legs exit	sleep after a bath	T wakes me up to talk about pastor	Pastor Short is having sex with Mama

DATE

EXERCISE	SETS	WEIGHT	REPS	GOALS	EXECUTION	JUSTIFY
regional softball championship	one	the world	two more chances before graduation	win	not win	distracted
batter up: me	one inning	the whole fucking team	one swing	home run	my elbow crushed by pitch	looking at Esperanza instead of the ball
meet medical professionals	round of Percocet	a few pills, an IV bag	hopefully more and more and more	stop the pain	just before the medicine works, every atom of the nurse's head spills out like rice	remember Esperanza wishing me good luck

DATE

EXERCISE	SETS	WEIGHT	REPS	GOALS	EXECUTION	JUSTIFY
surgery	a single morning	a nightmare	only if there is an infection later	bionic arm, super strength, invincibility	grogginess, immobility	T pushed the morphine button every time I blinked

DATE

EXERCISE	SETS	WEIGHT	REPS	GOALS	EXECUTION	JUSTIFY
meet grief counselor one-on-one	one	a thing I could've believed in	individual and group	1. discuss grief log progress 2. discuss possible obsessive-compulsive disorder	discuss college athletic scholarships and Title IX inequalities	grief counselor is a lesbian
meet grief counselor with Mama and T	one	sitting alone among nonbelievers	just twice before Mama called bullshit on therapy	1. discuss pain management 2. discuss Mama's new boyfriend	discuss dream about popping pimples	grief counselor is a dumbass

DATE

EXERCISE	SETS	WEIGHT	REPS	GOALS	EXECUTION	JUSTIFY
Esperanza visits in hospital	one	129 pounds, black hair wet from a shower, five foot ten and growing	just the one so far	be cool, look strong	get wet	Esperanza's voice is soft like paper sliding against itself

DATE

EXERCISE	SETS	WEIGHT	REPS	GOALS	EXECUTION	JUSTIFY
go home from hospital				feel more comfortable, less cold, smell less blood and chemicals	smell the weed from Mama's room, the strangeness of another man's presence	there is less there now for me and more elsewhere

A whole life empties out like rice on the floor.

Fat

When the PA removed the cast, it didn't smell as bad as I expected. The cast cracked off like a broken shell, my arm the tongue of a sea creature exposed, cold and vulnerable. As soon as it came off I slid from the noisy exam bed to leave, but there was more to do and the PA put up his hands in protest. I didn't get it, really, the cage door had been unlatched and I could go throw my skin under the sun, maybe even join the softball team again, although my sister, T, wouldn't let me. She waited by the car, so she could vape. Most bones heal well with treatment, I vaguely remember him saying when I was brought in. His breath smelled like red onions and honey-mustard salad dressing. After a bone breaks a blood clot seeps in around the halves. After a while a kind of prebone net grows inside the hematoma, slowly taking hold of the bone and pushing out the blood. Eventually the bone net solidifies into new bone and everything is fine. A seventy-mile-an-hour softball hit my elbow like cannon fire last spring. They gave me pain meds and surgery and pain meds and metal screws and more surgery and more pain meds and then nothing and more nothing until now.

"You've put on some weight," he said.

The PA's name was Paul or William or Paul William. I didn't look at his chest because I didn't look at people too often. Paul or William was white, with a spotty beard and shiny thinning hair cut close. He wasn't a man in a sexual sense to me, but his energy probably was supposed to be sexual. I hadn't gotten used to that thing that happens to people. I would feel it around Coach sometimes, not the desire to have sex but the reminder that it was possible, like storms are possible when clouds appear. Paul or William didn't know a lot of things. He didn't know why I was alone at the pediatrician's when all the other teenagers had their parents dutifully in tow. He didn't know my father died of sleep apnea the previous winter. He didn't know my mother was so depressed she had cashed the life insurance policy for half a million dollars and spent every day high as shit while me and T managed the household, and I personally had to listen to a grown man comment on my medically insignificant weight gain. Paul or William was new, meaning he was a well-intentioned ass hat.

I quit softball like T wanted, sat around all summer, but I hadn't noticed the change in my body. Perhaps a different kind of girl would've been hurt by that. A different kind of girl would've told her mother, who would have filed a complaint and exchanged letters with lawyers to feel all that could be done for her daughter's emotional fortress had been done. A different kind of girl would've given him the evil eye and silent treatment until he walked back the comment to something so unrecognizable that it becomes a spell that conjures a nurse to finish the appointment. A different kind of girl would've said fuck you and your eyebrow mole. A different kind of girl would've tried to seduce him to prove her worth and fall headfirst into a bucket of low self-esteem and thirty-seven minutes later, in the Wendy's parking lot with a cock in her mouth, feel for a brief moment victorious.

T had sex with Coach even after she made us quit the team. It still was mysterious. I couldn't call it love. I've seen the videos of what is supposed to happen and I still can't imagine it, sex with men. Men are like giant tortoises—big and round and dense and kind of cute in a slow ancient way. I don't mind men, but I just don't want to do them. I'd rather slide lettuce into their mouths and watch them chew.

Paul or William wasn't our doctor or even an actual doctor. After Daddy died our actual doctor met us one time at a physical to tell us he got a job in another state. He seemed so sad about it, the timing, that he would be going right after we lost our father, like it was such a cosmic tragedy or insult. He really overthought it. Me and T were like it's okay and it was okay, very okay, totally normal, but Dr. Lee was soggy eyed, apologizing over and over. It was a lot. Paul or William became the new normal. To be young and lack ambition seemed the new normal. He finished wiping down my arm and doing tests for mobility.

"You can exercise again now with more freedom. You used to be fit, you know."

That time was too much. I looked Paul or William in

the face hard and wanted to thump his right nipple and send a sting through his whole heart. The look on his face reminded me why I don't like to look at people, how simple they are; it's like they're made of soup cans stacked up and held together with Elmer's glue, dental floss, and hope. Their big chicken-noodle-soup heads will always crack open and say something stupid.

"I didn't mean it like that!" Paul or William said in a hurry. "I just remember you were an athlete, right? My nephew plays football now. He's okay"—he wobbled his hand in the air—"getting better. Plays receiver but should probably hold the line, doesn't have the hands for it."

I stopped looking at Paul or William, to be kind or maybe just to demand silence. This was the Kaiser Permanente in Long Beach, one city over and noisy. Nearly every seat in the waiting room was always filled. I met T outside. She looked like herself, face a perfect pear wrapped in the blue air from the vape. The palm trees in the landscaping sighed in the late morning breeze. I wanted a breakfast sandwich, some kind of potatoes, and an apple pie. She looked down at me and grabbed my elbow hard to see if it hurt. I didn't flinch, so she was satisfied.

"He called me fat," I told her.

She laughed, looked along my body, shrugged some, nodded some, kicked my calves lightly as if checking tire pressure, and said, "Yeah, kinda."

Lizard Sex

Lizards having sex is a lot like wrestling. On a trip to Phoenix visiting two of the aunties, I saw a ball of dirt on the wall that turned out to be two lizards going at it. I had to be maybe twelve and the idea of sex was fine, something distant and only interesting to adults, though I'd begun to intentionally touch my own body. Strange things would arouse me then and maybe now, like *Gilligan's Island*, all those odd white people on an island forever. It wasn't gay or straight or the parts that were supposed to be romantic. Skipper and Gilligan would turn me on sometimes, the way the skipper would beat Gilligan with his cap and smash it back on his own head. Who knows?

At Auntie Rae's house in the desert during July we didn't do much until the sun went down or barely came up. She had the nicest house of everybody we knew and made the drive from California to Arizona worth the sweat and gas. Walking out there was like being suspended in the mouth of a giant beast, the air became breath moving over us. We got to drink slushies and Capri Sun nonstop,

though, which I appreciated. Me and T went swimming
with the cousins. Auntie Rae's husband was Black while
Auntie Jackie's latest boyfriend was white. Auntie Jackie
had two mixed kids and Auntie Rae had all Black kids. Me
and T thought all of the cousins were kind of fucked-up
but just thought Arizona was like that. They didn't sound
quite like us, didn't play quite like us, but they weren't as
foreign as Auntie Tammy's kids in Alabama. They were a
whole bag of different accents, but we liked them better
than the Arizona ones. Sometimes the Black cousins teased
T and the mixed cousins for being lighter than the rest of
us, the bitter kind of teasing that is fused with hatred and
envy and resentment at the imaginary notion that there is
a difference of any significance at all. It was a feeling older
and bigger than anything we could hold on to, something
inherited in the way the adults talked about each other
and their children, like how Auntie Rae gave compliments
to the beauty of Auntie Jackie's kids with her lips turned
down like she tasted salt in her coffee. T would just do laps
and return underwater to grab us by the ankles and drag
us under, everyone laughing and drowning.

Mama was pretty much normal then, normal for
her but not quite for a mom. Me and T had been figuring that out. That there were different kinds of mamas
like there were different kinds of daddies. We had a really
good daddy. He was awake all the time and strong and
made us laugh and could do our hair. He was a mama in
a way. Other mamas did a lot of that, but they were less

strong and got tired easily because they were fat already. Our mama was more like us, a child, something to take care of except she was bigger than us and had power we didn't to drive cars and assign chores that didn't always make sense or make us fight each other for prizes that never manifested. She was a lot of work. And that was her normal, but I could see the way she held on to Daddy, leaned into him even when no one was looking or everybody was looking because it must've felt good. There had to be something going on that I couldn't quite see.

T decided to have a contest on who could do the best cannonball. We each took turns trying to stylistically fall into the pool. Two of the cousins tried to jump simultaneously and butted heads. There was blood weeping from an eyebrow, but T held a towel there and shushed away any tears so no one would get in trouble. It seemed important to keep the adults away from us. We were all in solidarity on that front. We learned from Daddy what to do when a kid gets hurt doing something stupid, you hold them as they shudder through pain and failure until the only energy left is peace. T did that and she looked grown to me then like she should have a house of her own and a car and a place to go in the mornings that makes her tired and glad to leave and go back to her house with kids playing video games on the carpet in the living room.

I saw the lizards on the brick wall fence while we were waiting for the blood to clot, a bandage, and pool time to continue. They were knotted together so tight it was hard to tell head from tail. It must've felt good to them in an invisible way. Just because I couldn't see it didn't mean more wasn't happening inside the body, churning up like hot water in a kettle, but I would not hear a screaming teapot as the climax, they could hold each other like that for only so long before it would be unbearable or just simply complete. Whatever electric collision of atoms or psychic energy happens in that lizard knot, I got turned on a little then too, probably in just the space between realizing I wasn't looking at mud and recognizing a fist-sized lump of lizard love. I threw one of the pool toys at them to break them up, to control the moment maybe. They didn't move. One of the cousins came over to see what I was doing, desperate for some action now that the hour turned to blood and pain. But I pushed him in the pool immediately to protect the lizards, to protect the feeling I had contracting in my own body, to rule over something in a space that felt on the edge of disorder, to keep it all to myself.

Dick Pic

When Pastor Short took us all to that fancy steak restaurant near the Staples Center, T got a dick pic from him. She didn't even have to be that sneaky about it. I often marveled to myself about T's ideas, her execution, plans that are always so magnificent and far away from my field of vision. I tried not to let her know how much I admired her, little sisters have to keep some dignity. Still, she amazed. Where I saw like an ant she saw like a hawk, a hawk with a treasure trove of penises preserved in digital format for a thousand years.

The week before we had to go to dinner, Mama had been nice to me and T, didn't order us to do chores that we were doing anyway, stayed relatively sober and quiet, bought juice and eggs herself instead of having things delivered or T pick them up. Then she dropped the news that the three of us would be having dinner out with Pastor on Saturday. Everything became clearer to me and T. Mama bought a whole outfit for me, made me wear the purple bra and a shirt and half tried to get me to wear a ridiculous skirt, but the look on my face must've been too much for her because it never made it more than a quarter out of the shopping bag before she turned away from me. I put on my jeans and didn't say anything else other than ask the name of the restaurant so I could look at the menu in advance.

I wore the diamond studs Daddy got me for my sixteenth birthday. T told me I looked nice and I almost kicked her before I realized she meant it. She'd been getting weird for a while, going all tender in the chest and sentimental, and it was annoying as hell. We all were handling death now in our own ways. I exercised and had poorly developed fantasies about girls, well, one girl. T had sex with our ex–softball coach we'd known for half our lives and catalogued pictures of his junk.

There were protesters outside of the restaurant when we pulled into the valet, wearing red and black and chanting with drums. Maybe they were challenging an immigration law or it was a Native American cultural demonstration. I couldn't tell. The signs weren't angled at me. A few people gathered in support or for entertainment.

Pastor Short was a big man but not at all fit. Our father could've fit inside of Pastor Short except would've busted out at the wrists and ankles. Daddy was long and lean like T. Pastor Short had to adjust the booth some to make room for his middle. He moved the heavy wooden table with ease, so I could tell he was flabby but strong, always slick like something old and oceanic. The restaurant was dimly lit and full of brick, wood, and amber light. Everyone looked like they were in Polaroids half-developed.

The time Mama had spent cultivating my new look hadn't been for the reasons I thought at first. I realized she didn't do my hair for me to touch me, to know me, to check the shape of my skull, but to prepare the room for him, for Pastor. Me and T were the set decorations. T wore a long wavy ponytail that week; it came down to her waist. I helped pick it out when she considered going shorter. She wore the diamond necklace she got for her sixteenth birthday, and it rested on her boobs and twinkled. She was pretty there and maybe all the time. I wouldn't know because she was such a loud, farting, coughing, screaming, arm-twisting taskmaster most of the time. That day she sat like a portrait. Perfect.

Mama had her hand on Pastor Short's thigh through most of dinner, so ate with one hand only. I ordered salmon, which seemed appropriate if I had to look at Pastor. Eating something that he seemed related to felt the best defense against his very being and a way to claim solidarity with T. Whenever I glanced at T during dinner she seemed far away; it was a look I knew well and I wondered just how the world was opening itself to her. Whenever I glanced at Pastor he was trying to look just left of T's boobs and back to Mama.

Pastor Short asked us about school and such to be polite. We answered the same, fine, fine. I had been hanging out with Esperanza more, taking more strange fighting classes that were starting to feel good, it was the only physical contact with anyone I had at the time, the legs of that old lady (Barb) and holding a punching bag for Esperanza on occasion. We hung out at her house once too, but that was weirder than rubbing legs with that old lady, Barb. Esperanza insisted I come in through her window and wouldn't let me use the bathroom. She looked apologetic the whole time I had to hold it while nineties sci-fi television episodes streamed on her laptop for us.

The protesters were getting louder and closer to the windows of the restaurant. There was something angry and desperate in the chanting. I wondered if it had always been like that, the chanting over centuries, all the way back to the beginning. Were the drums ever happy? I wondered what happened to them, to us, over generations that painfully strained the vocal cords into what we heard then. Maybe I just heard it all wrong.

At some point everyone went to the restroom individually, but T timed it just right so that she was able to be alone with Pastor Short away from us in the dungeon-like hallways that led to the facilities. It still baffles me how a man will just share his privates so willy-nilly without lengthy debate or consideration or negotiation. I asked T when we were at home. Pastor refused the offer Mama made for him to stay for a glass of wine, which meant they would just go alone in the bedroom for a few hours before he crept out at around 1:00 a.m. He dropped us all off in a hurry. T told me she asked to see it and he said okay. I fell down laughing.

"Just, Okay!" I said, mocking Pastor Short's voice.

"Like, sure. Thank you very much for the inquiry. You wanna see my dick in the name of the Father, the Son, and the Holy Ghost? And so shall it be given unto thee."

It was crazy, but I was learning, and the lessons were bizarre. T tried to shush me through her own laughter. She knew it would be that easy, and I felt a little ill and the ground moved under me because of that. Still, we were laughing, and with all this new knowledge and treasure there seemed opportunities.

Black Communion

I t was Communion day when Pastor Short announced before the congregation his engagement to a woman who was not our mother. I learned people just feed the possessions of the dead to Goodwill so they don't sprout bad dreams that pretend to be memories. Instead of doing our little-by-little Sunday donations of Daddy's clothes, we went to church. Communion was my favorite religious activity. We got to eat our God and drink His blood once a month. Christians are something else, but I can't deny that it is a little bit empowering to think we can consume our Creator, and He'd be totally cool with it.

The ritual of getting dressed exhausted me, the dresses and the pumps, and the matching sling purses. I hated it. T loved it. She loved the show, a pageant of sinners all powdery and polished, ready to be doused with Jesus' bucket of forgiveness even though she never stayed awake for half of it. When we left for church, Mama's makeup looked like something to peel off, far too light, leaving the trunk of her neck dark. We never said anything. At least she was getting out of the house.

Sister Bloom read the announcements: couples' ministry meeting times, vacation Bible study schedule, building fund goals, etc. Out of all that BS she left off a lot of the good stuff. Still, I was waiting on the main event.

Catholics have a different process, from what I saw on TV. They have Communion every week and line up while a priest hand-delivers a wafer directly into their mouths, one at a time. It doesn't even stop there. They then drink from the same cup of juice. There was no way I would get all dressed up for Pastor Short to slide an oyster cracker with his bare walrus fingers onto my tongue. GTFOH.

Sister Bloom forgot to mention that Pastor Short had been fornicating with our mother for half a year since Daddy died. Second, she forgot to mention the dick pic Pastor Short sent to my sister, T. Then Sister Bloom forgot to mention that once T got that dick pic he'd given up a lot of power and could never get it back, so he stopped coming over more and more until his absence forced Mama to actually go to church again and confront him. Lastly, Sister Bloom failed to mention that Pastor Short was a greasy-lipped hypocrite, so I was like, Whatever, lady. You work on your building fund.

T ate and drank her Sacrament before the big moment because she always forgot or never cared and was ready to fall into her creepy sleep again, sitting straight up with her eyes half-open like a basset hound in a floral dress. I saved my Communion until after everyone else tossed back their cups.

Jesus tastes like low-sodium saltines and Welch's grape juice and was probably into carbs. Mama's makeup had blended well over the hours, turning her face into a daub of peanut butter. I considered telling her that Pastor Short's new fiancée was ugly, which was true, but I hadn't developed a habit of talking to my mother. We weren't that kind of family. She'd been gripping the pews tightly for a while as if trying to balance herself, screaming beautifully in silence. I really thought I should say something. After the juice came the hymn, "I Know It Was the Blood," the most jubilant chant about bathing in the vital fluids of a deity ever written; it had the cadence and delight of nursery rhymes, though the irony on the people was not lost, a song and dance of the conquerors and the conquered, a kind of covenant beyond the moment to something deep into the future with a fist around the past.

Once the music was in full ecstasy, Mama made a sound. She said, "Huh," with her whole chest, a note between scorn and epiphany. Then I said it too, except I was all scorn and no epiphany. Maybe it was the sugar and liquid dye and pureed fruit or the grit of salt and flour on our tongues that evoked sudden calm. The church was disproportionately women, most of the men tending to the altar, circling the pastor while the audience of women with hands stretched out propped up the men in their elevation to heaven.

I only imitated her revelation at the time, but my

mother had figured it out that at any moment we women could remove our hands from the air, take back our obedience, our bodies, swallow our devotion, and the whole establishment would cave in like hollow bread. She understood how the price we pay to worship is grave and will tax us to the marrow, how the dead stay dead and it is the living who will frighten, astonish, and disappoint. I always saved my Sacrament because I wanted to eat the last of our God my own way.

In the Counselor's Waiting Room with No Wi-Fi

DOWN

2. Watching Coach exercise in the morning when no one else was on campus yet became a mystical experience like watching this creature close-up in flight, should not be possible according to physicists, but there it is, natural as a rainbow.

3. The thing each girl on the softball team possesses but can't find without me and T.

5. Those who liked being told what to do by Coach under any situation. Don't be trashy, Brooks. Find a can for that can, Smith. They loved being called by their last names, found it challenging or endearing.

6. How I used to feel in the mornings before a game.

7. The most primitive, universal, timeless, essential, and risky exercise.

9. The boys were jealous and studious. They studied Coach's movement and imitated him, causing this and testosterone to explode in the air like swarms of midges.

11. An act performed during PE and lunch. A territorial marking done through motion, declaration of being, a summoning of bodies together, the most accurate test of physical intelligence.

12. The number-one thing I missed after quitting softball with my sister, T, to avoid Coach—the careful washing after practice, the cold cycle to preserve the color, the hand-drying and ironing, the green stripe down the side with not a single ripple.

14. The outcome of most games when T and I played. The team looked impeccable, performed much the same. T had the image, I the strength.

ACROSS

1. The boys' nickname for Coach. They mocked his hairline, low to the eyebrows, quick to point out something bearlike about his face, a dark nose set in a brown backdrop.

4. Because his upper body significantly outweighed his lower limbs, Coach resembles this bird while running, chest puffed, arms tucked close to the torso like he held important files there.

8. When talking to the counselor about Coach's inappropriate/ criminal behavior I could tell she wanted to smoke. Her eyes reminded me of these pointy tools of sinister men in white who can see a child bleed and cry and suddenly feel they've done a good job.

10. The type of people who found Coach attractive.

13. According to T, this is most similar to sex with Coach. "It's like being hot and sick under a huge blanket."

15. Coach treated the girls like these animals, which are some- times eaten or mutilated by assholes with more power than cuteness; they get drowned by sociopathic preteens or develop mange or when lucky lose an eyeball to a flock of braver-than-most seagulls in an alley, fighting over a corn chip. They are very cute, and cute can get you killed.

16. The energy that surrounded Coach could not be dismissed among the girls and boys; it got hold of you from the inside out like a drumbeat stuck in your head.

Halloween

Esperanza and me saw a car following a girl while riding back from jiujitsu practice. We were on our bikes and took Central all the way back down to the neighborhood. It was a Honda, dark green like a rental, like something nobody picks out for themselves but got because they thought it looked normal. The girl was just a few years younger than us, probably, small and thin like an uncooked pretzel in purple pants and T-shirt. She was on her phone, looked nervous, and I could feel the pace in Esperanza's pedaling slow down. So I slowed down too.

Central is usually a busy street, but not that time of day, late October near sunset on a weekday. Everybody who should be home was home already. We passed the cemetery that butts up against the elementary school. One car passed, then no cars. Invisible birds gossiped about each other from the trees. The bike ride plus actual jiujitsu practice was three hours of physical activity. Esperanza wanted to stop for Now and Laters, but I wanted a burrito. The car and the girl drifted farther away and then the girl turned onto Caldwell. The car followed. Now and Laters are the worst candy and will yank a filling out or a whole tooth depending on the mouth we're talking about. Esperanza pronounced them more like *annihilators* the way everybody else did.

Noemi had been taking turns kicking our asses for weeks. We were not good, practically speaking. I was strong enough to hold my ground, make myself heavy and hard to turn, but against Noemi's skill it meant nothing. Noemi was like a crocodile. She'd tuck her arms close to her body and smile like some mad ancient mini-dinosaur just waiting for us to try something that would fail. Then she snapped, and in seconds Esperanza would be colliding with the floor or I'd have a shoulder joint about to dislodge. It hurt so bad but was beautiful.

Esperanza had bigger wheels than I, a whole bigger bike, actually. Mine was made for kids or grown-ass men who thought they were kids and liked to fling themselves upside down just to feel something. The bigger wheels made her faster, so it was strange to be in the lead for once as we rode.

That day Noemi had jammed her finger on something unrelated to BJJ at all and couldn't participate. She just coached me and Esperanza on how to escape from front-facing chokes. I had to practice grabbing Esperanza by the throat over and over. Esperanza kept telling me to make it tighter, tighter, tighter. When I thought it was way too much and was about to let go she said okay, good.

It wasn't cold yet. October was like that. The trees were giving up their color, but it wasn't like TV with the piles of leaves that dogs jumped in and the cut of an icy breeze. The air here could get humid and balmy even if the stores wanted to sell us pumpkin-colored sweaters and brown leather boots. We rode home in our T-shirts, the short sleeves rolled up under our pits.

To this day I feel like perverts drive Hondas. The little girl had been out of sight for too long, and the car too. I wasn't afraid like Esperanza yet; it didn't occur to me that I should've been until I saw her lean forward on her bike and begin to pedal past me. Sometimes it's the witnessing of a horror story that makes us forget we're in one. She pedaled for the life of the little girl and our own. I pedaled just to keep up. Back then I had no imagination for the worst of us, those who take and take and stretch the tender parts of life to the point of breaking.

I saw a play once as a kid about a detective bear that solved mysteries. I used to think about crime that way for a long time, like a child in a theater safely surrounded by adults who keep the danger far away on a stage. Criminals weren't actual people anymore; they were impostors playing a part, monsters inside of a human husk to hide their true selves, their buckled skin, hot dumpster breath, stained cotton balls for eyes, and vinegar sweat. It doesn't take long to realize that it isn't like that at all.

We pedaled and pedaled for only seconds before we stopped. We stopped because the little girl was running toward us now. She'd come back from around the corner

to the silent main street, where there was nothing but our
heartbeats and the complaints of birds in the air. I was
ready to die, not for the little girl but for Esperanza, because Esperanza chewed her dangerous candy, walked into
bruises day after day, and demanded that I try to squeeze
the life from her just to test her worth. I knew as strong as
we were, as fast as we were, we were still very young and
in relation to whoever was in that Honda probably very
small and not at all like Noemi, made hard as a needle by
the world. So I readied myself for death.

We stopped and held our ground while the girl made
it to us and paused in between our bikes, looking over her
shoulder as the car slowly approached. I wanted the car
to careen into the curb and then a corpse stumble out of
the passenger side and a greasy alien with a mouth like
a lamprey eel and arms long as my whole body to burst
from the windshield. But villains never look the way they
should. Threats are often surprising and unannounced, so
it takes a lot of people to protect one another, especially
little girls. The car sped off and even though all of our eyes
watched it go, we never saw the driver. Just like that we
were alone, the three of us. The day faded fast right before
the gold streetlights lit up the sidewalk. We had the dusk
to ourselves and moved exhausted again through time as
if the shapes of the night could be anything we wanted.

Quiz

Match the teacher to the description, direct quote, and unsaid thing.

1. Dr. Bontemps
   (U.S. Government)
   _____

2. Coach Watson
   (PE/Softball Instructor)
   _____

3. Ms. Harris
   (French/Spanish)
   _____

4. Mrs. Washington
   (Health and Wellness)
   _____

A. Distributes a basket of bananas and condoms once a semester with full-color photos of STIs in bloom: our total comprehensive sex education.

B. Selective in his predatory obsession with certain girl athletes; can do thirty pull-ups in a row and insists on demonstrating weekly.

C. Chews and pops bubble gum all period, the mass explodes over her matte-purple lipstick like a bladder full of air over and over.

D. A true hotep motherfucker, always eating organic raw almonds and cranking his lips down at one thing or another from the girls' hairstyles to our cheese and crackers.

5. Mr. Strauss
   (Spanish)
   _____

6. Coach Hales
   (PE/Wrestling)
   _____

7. Ms. Williams
   (AP English)
   _____

E. White South African, bald, pale
   like a peanut salesman in a
   black-and-white movie.

F. One of few lingering members
   of a previous generation of
   white faculty who now find
   themselves in a Black and brown
   institution—super old, with the
   rounded spine of an armadillo.

G. Arms and head like a
   Tyrannosaurus rex with
   perpetually droopy eyes like
   she will burst into apology for
   something but never does.

- -

1. Dr. Bontemps
   _____

2. Coach Watson
   _____

3. Ms. Harris
   _____

4. Mrs. Washington
   _____

5. Mr. Strauss
   _____

A. "Your accent marks are
   backwards. Wait, they're fine.
   Just ask me where the damn
   bathroom is!"

B. "Don't eat your own dicks,
   people!"

C. "I am an African American too."

D. "Slavery on paper ended in 1864,
   but slavery of the Black mind is
   big business today!"

E. "James Baldwin said . . ."

6. Coach Hales
_____

F. "Stop dragging your asses. Knees up!"

7. Ms. Williams
_____

G. "It's not football!"

- -

1. Dr. Bontemps
_____

A. "The Black woman is a queen, but they insist on putting the artificial scraps of white and Asian capitalism on their crowns."

2. Coach Watson
_____

B. "The girl is going to be fat. Most of them, probably. They'll all look like hell in ten years, tops. Lazy. Won't get anything done without being told."

3. Ms. Harris
_____

C. "Cal State Dominguez Hills is hiring adjuncts for the fall."

4. Mrs. Washington
_____

D. "The whole goddamn world thinks the only sports that matter have a fucking ball."

5. Mr. Strauss
_____

E. "I'm not even supposed to teach Spanish."

6. Coach Hales
_____

F. "Every year the brains get smaller, the legs longer, and the tits bigger. There has to be some kind of conspiracy. Something is in the milk."

7. Ms. Williams
_____

G. "I offer kinship though we are not the same, not today or tomorrow. I know more of the world than you, how much cruelty awaits no matter what we say or do."

Menstruation

When me, T, and Mama are all on our periods, things get volatile. Women menstruating at the same time is a myth except when it's not. Sudden irrational displays of emotion during PMS are also a myth but happen from time to time. Mama threw a shoe at us one of those times. White laces propelled up and out, spiraling like knotted antennae from the sneaker, whizzing out of the hall in an arc, a teeny-tiny helicopter hunting over a city, a warning shot. She had the latent power of a full-grown woman, which we figured made no difference because she was just old and out of shape. It made all the difference.

I used to get away with the big maxi pads in softball. The uniforms of wrestling were not so forgiving. Even with undershorts the outline of the pad came through like a surfboard. T gave me a tampon and assured me it had nothing to do with virginity and all those other girls were dumbasses. She left me alone in the bathroom. I half read the instructions and didn't understand the difference between applicator and tampon; they were one and the same and I figured everything had to go in and stay there.

The entire tampon and applicator rested in my vagina like a ballpoint pen when the bone assignment was explained. I held still as possible, curious about the pain women had to have. We needed to go to a butcher for this one, Ms. Lancaster explained. Buy a pork or beef bone, a femur, have the butcher saw it in half lengthwise, tip him for the extra effort, boil the halves for x amount of time, then let them dry or wash them off, but that didn't make sense, and print out pieces of paper, which also didn't make sense, and color the bone in a code of some kind. I took notes quickly but still too slowly to get all of the details. The assignment seemed illicit and creepy, with the promise of something beautiful at the end, a colored code, a rainbow after such barbarity. I loved it. I loved that an animal would give up its bones for me to play with in my kitchen then prepare a design, cast labels on the parts like Adam.

T half caught the other shoe Mama threw right at her, held back like a grenade; half caught, half absorbed the impact right in the chest and collarbone, her reflexes whip quick. The third rolled sideways at T, a boot. I deflected it with a smack, didn't bother to catch it, a mistake really, the ammunition returned. This went on for three more rounds in silence, no screaming, no arguing, just the swing of footwear colliding against palms, meaty sounds from the rubber, nylon, and skin as it all tumbled through the air.

Science kept me alert, the smells of formaldehyde-laden desks half cleaned for decades, enormous black desks with a special chemical coating, dinged and chipped and scratched. They let me do the dirty work, trusted me to peel the gladius from the baby squid, extract the pigeon brain (difficult; one girl slit her nail with a scalpel on the skull), and line them up on a tray. Now I had a bone to work with all to myself.

Mama ran out of breath and gave up the exercise or punishment and retreated to a pot of coffee. No one died. I hated her. I appreciated her. In the abrupt end to the weird conversation between T and Mama and me, one thing rose from the breath of it, a shapeless feeling that scratched and whistled too loud to let anybody take a nap.

When I told T the plastic made the tampon more than uncomfortable, her eyes jostled in her head like gelatin, the white tissue layered around the deep red rippled. Glee took over her whole body, and I realized I'd been making a painful, messy error. I knew not to tell her about the bone because I wanted that for me and no one else. Her laughter struck me as unbelievable, like raising a body from the dead, the kind of miracle better left in our past because to perform it now only raises questions we can't be bothered to ask.

Ambien and Brown Liquor

Me and T went to the Denny's across from the hospital at three in the morning the night Mama tried to kill herself. T ordered a BLT sandwich on sourdough with fries. I got the pancake breakfast with eggs sunny-side up, hash browns, and bacon. The waitress was good. Never asked us how we were doing, just punctuated all of her sentences with "sweetie." What can I get you, sweetie? Anything to drink, sweetie? Coming right up, sweetie.

"Why didn't you get the chocolate ones like always?" T asked.

"I'm trying out the blueberry."

She sat back in the booth like it was really something to think about, the blueberry pancakes versus the chocolate pancakes with the whipped-cream smiley face. Certainly, this was not a time for smiles in our food, and she understood that after I did. Maybe figuring that out late was the problem she had to consider so deeply. We should've been covered in blood. We hadn't been taught the proper signs of death, how it doesn't lurk in dark robes or burst from a warrior's chest in battle or appear as the slow-motion spray of brain matter and other vital organs scattered in the wind like dandelion fluff. That would've made more sense than looking the way we always look except in the face. T looked old as shit. Maybe we both did. Girls our age usually showed up at diners in the middle of the night coming down off pills and wine coolers after being molested for hours on a dance floor.

"You look like Auntie Tammy," I told her.

"Fuck you," she said with a laugh.

It was dark outside and quiet, with a thin fog that made the streetlights fuzzy and jittery. Only two other groups were in the entire restaurant, which was large enough to hold fifty or a hundred, I don't know. A few tables away a family waited, two women, a youngish man, and a girl with a pink balloon tied to her wrist asleep in one of the women's laps. The balloon hovered above them all, singular and swaying in the air-conditioning. In the other aisle was a couple, two older men, sad like us but a little different. They ate soup and drank ice water with lemon. All of these people should've been covered in blood, dried and full of tissue and matted hair. It should be fresh too, running in places from wounds always recently torn open and from the dead that drip onto them. The droopy men and the heavy women and the little girl with her shoe about to fall off her foot as she drooled on the woman's lap, all of them should've been covered in blood. Then the waitress came over and brought our coffee, she too awash in death, smiling behind the steam from the mugs.

"Here you go, sweeties."

I imagined the coagulated masses of torn flesh dropping into the cups from her chin like red cubes of sugar.

"Thank you," we said.

I remember going to the emergency room as a kid after an ant crawled into my ear and wouldn't come out. Mama held my head under the faucet while I cried, but nothing washed out. "It's in there!" I yelled over and over, hearing it bang and buzz around inside me like a mad tiny chef cooking stir-fry.

T looked up at me, then she looked out at the street. She held her coffee like a woman who had lived a lifetime and earned every sip.

"In the zombie apocalypse, would you kill me if I got bit?" I asked T.

She sweetened her coffee. Tasted it. Then sweetened it some more.

"Or what?" she asked.

"Or just let me turn?"

"Would you try to eat me?"

"Of course."

I took a bite of bacon and slit the eggs with my fork so the yolk ran into the hash browns.

T leaned forward with her elbows on the table and looked out into the dark empty streets. No cars passed. No people passed. There was nothing out there.

"How would you want me to kill you, then?"

"I don't care if it hurts some."

"Really?"

"Yeah, that's fine."

"I'd try to not make it hurt, though."

"So you would kill me?"

I dropped my fork. She squirted ketchup on her fries and began to eat.

"Is that a problem? You seem like you want it, and a lot of times you deserve it. I would just have to remember how annoying you are and then just boom."

We had very little practice with death before that year, and then the bitch began outperforming itself all around us. First no one was dead, then everyone seemed to be gone or leaving. Life felt like the mystery. All of the people around us acted as if they were alive when really they were closer to the end than they'd like to think. None of the dead and dying we knew looked like they were supposed to.

"So, you'd shoot me? Your favorite sister?"

"My only sister, and maybe. Do we get guns in this movie?"

"It's not a movie. I just want to know what to expect."

"Would you kill me, then?"

"No!"

"What? You'd just let me run around all gross and eat people."

"Yes!"

"That's crazy."

She sipped her supersweet coffee and seemed to begin aging backward a little. I was glad for that. I saw T more in that moment, and maybe I would kill her in the zombie apocalypse if she looked more like T, pretty, her dark eyes cutting deep into whatever she stared at. Maybe I would just let her die like that with that face.

"Right now," T said. "You have to promise to shoot me in the fucking face if I get bit by a fucking zombie. I do not want to live forever as a rotting chest-bones-out, jaw-swinging corpse."

I laughed at her imitating a zombie jaw.

"Do that again."

She did. I laughed harder. The men with the soup got up to pay their bill. The little girl was awake and sipping orange juice from a child's cup.

"Look," she said. "Promise. I would kill you, then kill myself, so we wouldn't have to deal with any of it."

"But what if there's a cure? You just popped us both and the next day they announce free cures for everybody recently infected, and we're all dead and shit."

T smiled.

"Well, that would be a problem."

"Yes, a problem!"

"But we're dead, so it wouldn't matter. Dead people don't have problems."

She reached over with her fork and took a piece of pancake.

"These aren't as good as the chocolate ones."

"You just wanted me to get those so you could have some."

She ate another piece, then another, and quit trying to enjoy her terrible coffee. T liked to eat her sugar rather than drink it. We waited in the car until the sun came up before going back into the hospital. The most frightening things that eat up our lives can't be seen—simple bacteria, free radicals, cholesterol, time, protein deficiencies, cortisol, vanity, ambition, carcinogens, love, and all the erratic chemicals of grief and abandonment. T had found Mama on the sofa after coming home late. I'd been asleep for a while when I heard T screaming and screaming as if there had been a massacre, blood everywhere and nowhere. Our mother rested the whole day after having a tube inserted into her stomach to siphon the contents. Because she arrived unconscious they gave her a tracheal intubation to make sure she didn't inhale the poisons during extraction. When I had the ant removed the doctor smiled in my face, and asked if I wanted to keep it. I thought they might bottle up the juices from Mama's belly and ask if we wanted to take them home, but that didn't happen. We left with no proof at all.

Parthenogenesis

Somebody thought it was a good idea to take a family vacation after Mama tried to kill herself: San Diego. By some miracle of incompetence no one came for me and T right away, to take two nearly grown teenage girls from the jaws of maternal dysfunction. T said that level of extra was for white kids. So instead we ended up on a two-hour road trip south. San Diego, the yellowest city I'd ever seen, totally sunbleached, all the buildings, old and new, dipped in Mission-style architecture like an ice cream in adobe sprinkles. It was ridiculous.

T had been acting like a snatch-face *c*-word from the start. I'd never seen her so eager to go anywhere since before Daddy died. This was going to be our first vacation with just Mama, and knowing that woman I did not expect great things. But T, my goodness, the rushing and the shouting—get in the shower, put on your clothes, don't leave your hair like that, brush your goddamn teeth, help carry the cooler! Mama never touched me unless it was to tug and twist on my hair until it looked somewhat satisfying to us both. When she heard T yell at me she came over with a jar of product and a comb. It hurt the usual way and then it didn't. I wanted to cut it all off the way women do when they get divorced. I wanted to divorce my mother and her genetic code and her self-hate and her addictions and her disregard for her own beauty, her own body. I was done before we got in the car.

Things were going well for me, I had a wrestling match coming up, friends, more than friends even, and the two of them just plucked me out of it, root and all. Eventually we stopped talking, turned the radio off in the car, and just rode into the resort driveway in complete silence. I got out first for some fresh air. It smelled beachy and tropical, the artificial tropical that comes in tubes of sunblock or a tray of mai tais. All-inclusive, the receptionist repeated, whatever that meant. Mama had a lot of insurance money to spend and no idea what she was buying, apparently. There were other families checking in, men in khaki shorts and women in sunglasses so large they looked like giant flies wearing sundresses. Short brown and pink people struggling with luggage and no sense of direction, and that one Viking-looking couple that walked out of the elevator and out of the sliding glass doors to some other destiny. Then there was us: cranky, saggy eyed, hungry, grieving, and alone. With all T's shouting we still looked terribly unprepared for family fun by the beach. I had on a sweat suit with socks and flip-flops, T had on enough jewelry to use as armor in a war, and Mama had on a faux-leather jacket.

Everything about us said we did not know what the hell we were doing. The receptionist said all-inclusive for the twelfth time to clarify a point Mama refused to embrace, then recited a list of amenities, including six restaurants, a spa, an indoor space simulator, and an aquarium.

T packed all those sodas and water like we were going hiking at a park with Daddy. We didn't need any of it here. We ate horrible burgers that came with an unrequested pineapple on the meat for no goddamn reason, then went to the aquarium. A guided tour was in progress that we joined just in time to reach the manta ray exhibit. Six or seven little stingrays wide and flat as dinner plates scuttled along the sand. Guests were allowed to touch the little guys, which I thought a bad idea. A little blond boy insisted on trying to poke them in the exact manner the guide told him not to and had to be forcibly removed by a similar-looking man, a pattern he'd walk his whole life. Me and Mama looked at each other and rolled up our sleeves, then reached in hands flat like we were supposed to. The creatures came to us and slid like beaded glass under our fingers. She almost smiled then, eager to touch this strange little thing in this faraway place, and I realized I didn't know her at all. T didn't touch the stingrays and was glad to move on to the shark tank, which I will never forget.

Apparently there is a thing that can happen to some animals, spontaneous births, parthenogenesis, right out of ancient mythology, Zeus and Athena, the guide said. Their tank held only female sharks, but one Sunday evening a shark gave birth to eleven babies all on her own.

The guide spoke as if it were science, nature, the divine, and a curse. For a second lots of the women chuckled and nudged their men and felt a kind of pride where I felt immense terror. The thin guide in her bright-orange lipstick continued, parthenogenesis is a kind of self-cloning, the babies are identical to the mother genetically with minor differences here and there. Unfortunately, the babies are usually not well. I felt it coming, the grand joke this kind of singular motherhood represented. The babies are usually deformed, the guide said significantly, or stillborn altogether. Call it a panic attack, call it the heebie-jeebies, whatever it was I couldn't breathe well, even the feel of fabric on my abdomen made me shudder, and I had to leave before hearing anything else.

The hall between the shark tank and the hands-on exhibit was peaceful, dark, and empty. Someone spun me around so fast I almost put them in a choke hold, but it was just T. She held me by the collar and was at the point of crying. I got scared, figured Mama did something crazy again. In an instant I imagined her keeled over at the bar or half-submerged in the shore like a seashell, mouth and nose filled with sand, or in the shark tank, naked and drowned, wide-eyed with head and limbs tucked close to her like a fetus. But it was none of those things. Mama was just beyond T, gazing like she always did, quiet, locked in whatever past drove her to this moment that she couldn't go beyond. And there was T, looking at me like I might not be there. The shark talk messed you up too, I said. She laughed a little and let me go.

San Di-fucking-ego, a whole-ass mess. I'd come to find out that all-inclusive meant you got to eat and drink anything all day—crab legs, shrimp, steak skewers, chicken tacos, ribs, lasagna, and if you flirt with the young attendants they'll bring you endless piña coladas on the artificial dock at sunset while your drunk mother and sister cry on your shoulder, everyone not knowing which of us came first or if anyone would live through the night.

'Tis the Season

This was our first Christmas without Daddy, and living through all of the days leading up to it felt like marching up a rocky hill in flip-flops. T and I cried our hardest on December 4 while Mama was passed out on edibles. We loved Christmas and thought we would have to say goodbye to all of it because Daddy died and didn't leave us instructions. He was our Christmas guru, hanger of lights, cooker of hams, dancer to Motown carols sweet and salty like a mall pretzel on the last shopping day of the year. Now we were walking into haunted houses, ghosts everywhere.

Around December 10 we were handling things our own way. Mama got sentimental and invited Auntie Tammy all the way from Alabama to have dinner with us. T became a kitchen bitchhole, obsessing over cookies and dinner planning. She forced me to taste-test raw batter and sauces every evening after school. The salted caramel chocolate chunk cookie batter was the best. I did the lights. I tried to do the lights. The month was half-spent and I had only two bushes, a tree trunk, and a blinking train set working

on the front where there used to be an enviable display of
American holiday dick swinging. Ms. Holland spotted me
struggling to set up a ladder and called to me from across
the street.

Ms. Holland is a witch and sells candy to the neighborhood kids all year long, even during Christmas. She will
fuck you up if you try to steal from her, though, no matter
your age or size or your parents: bam, open palm to the
ear. Open palm because Ms. Holland couldn't make a true
fist. She had fingernails eleven inches long on each hand,
even the thumb. When she was younger she had them
way longer, multiple feet, broke a record. There's a picture of her in a book somewhere with her two grown sons
and daughter standing around her like a queen's court or
something.

When I heard Ms. Holland call, I knew I had to get
down from the ladder and go over to her. She wouldn't
tolerate a conversation in muffled shouts across the street
even though I still had forty thousand unplugged strings of
lights to identify, separate, and curse. I crossed the street
and stepped around the huge nearly dead palm tree absorb-
ing her front yard. Ms. Holland didn't celebrate Christmas,
far as I could tell, no fake garland, no paper Santa, no Styro-
foam holly that chips so much it looks like cereal, no smell
of collard greens or mac 'n' cheese or buttery dinner rolls
or cranberry sauces slick from the can ever came from her
house. I was surprised when she gave me a basket of as-
sorted meats and cheeses, then said it was for our family.
I chocked it up to late death food. Better than a casserole

any day, except the sausages looked better than they tasted. Ms. Holland offered to have one of her sons help me with the lights while she supervised, which I accepted. She also offered to read my cards, as in tarot cards, which I declined. She said tarot is an important science. I thanked her for the basket.

Actual Christmas dinner went as well as expected, meaning a fistfight and broken table. We had Auntie Tammy, Uncle Lou, and their two sons John and Isaiah. John and Isaiah were sixteen-year-old twins with bad attitudes and really good manners. They called Mama ma'am all day long and me and T couldn't handle it, so we avoided them as much as possible. Auntie Tammy insisted on taking over the kitchen from T and made chitterlings (aka shitlins). I thought something had died, they smelled so bad. Everyone except me and T did not seem to notice that the entire house smelled like literal poop. Auntie Tammy apparently did not make enough chitterlings because after a brief pause in conversation we noticed Uncle Lou staring at Isaiah and Isaiah staring back, then Uncle Lou grabbed Isaiah by the shirt and they went tumbling together across the kitchen. Everyone stood up away from the table when they crashed into it. Everything on the floor, including whatever personal battle they'd probably been fighting since birth the way men and sons do sometimes. Me and T went outside and ate cookies on the porch. She told me the lights looked nice, and we didn't feel like crying the way we thought we would. The steep hill to Christmas Day wasn't all that bad, kind of plateaued when T figured out the salted caramel chocolate chunk recipe. We ate our ghosts and settled our nerves, watching the neighborhood blink to life.

When Daddy was alive we would watch that barefoot Bruce Willis movie and eat strawberry ice cream on the floor before going to bed. Needles from the live tree that dried out too soon scattered on the carpet. I don't know why they call it a live tree when it is so very dead that it's decomposing before our eyes. Sometimes I would wake up already in bed and not remember being carried in there. It was frightening to lose time and space like that even though later I figured out what had happened.

I don't know if I've seen that picture of Ms. Holland or I imagined it. I've seen her kids, grown men but still kind of simple. They're always bringing her packages and groceries, running her errands while she sits and opens doors and arranges candy. They never seem that happy, though, but kind of locked in their routine like they couldn't leave it if they wanted to. I had a dream of Ms. Holland running her long-nailed hands along my head. I'd been shaved bald and she spoke of ghosts and sausages and I was running an Olympic marathon.

Answer Sheet

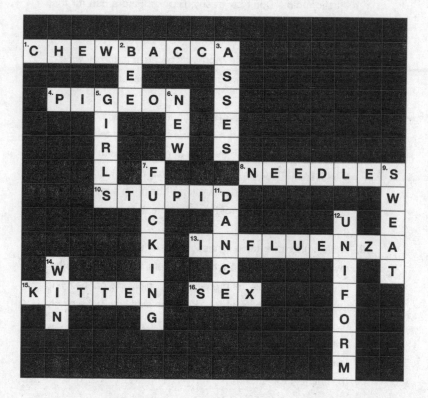

DOWN

2. Watching Coach exercise in the morning when no one else was on campus yet became a mystical experience like watching this creature close-up in flight, should not be possible according to physicists, but there it is, natural as a rainbow: bee.

3. The thing each girl on the softball team possesses but can't find without me and T: asses.

5. Those who liked being told what to do by Coach under any situation: girls. Don't be trashy, Brooks. Find a can for that can, Smith. They loved being called by their last names, found it challenging or endearing.

6. How I used to feel in the mornings before a game: new.

7. The most primitive, universal, timeless, essential, and risky exercise: fucking.

9. The boys were jealous and studious. They studied Coach's movement and imitated him, causing this and testosterone to explode in the air like swarms of midges: sweat.

11. An act performed during PE and lunch. A territorial marking done through motion, declaration of being, a summoning of bodies together, the most accurate test of physical intelligence: dance.

12. The number-one thing I missed after quitting softball with my sister, T, to avoid Coach—the careful washing after practice, the cold cycle to preserve the color, the hand-drying and ironing, the green stripe down the side with not a single ripple: uniform.

14. The outcome of most games when T and I played: win. The team looked impeccable, performed much the same. T had the image, I the strength.

ACROSS

1. The boys' nickname for Coach. They mocked his hairline, low to the eyebrows, quick to point out something bearlike about his face, a dark nose set in a brown backdrop: Chewbacca.

4. Because his upper body significantly outweighed his lower limbs, Coach resembles this bird while running, chest puffed, arms tucked close to the torso like he held important files there: pigeon.

8. When talking to the counselor about Coach's inappropriate/criminal behavior I could tell she wanted to smoke. Her eyes reminded me of these pointy tools of sinister men in white who can see a child bleed and cry and suddenly feel they've done a good job: needles.

10. The type of people who found Coach attractive: stupid.

13. According to T, this is most similar to sex with Coach: influenza. "It's like being hot and sick under a huge blanket."

15. Coach treated the girls like these animals, which are sometimes eaten or mutilated by assholes with more power than cuteness; they get drowned by sociopathic preteens or develop mange or when lucky lose an eyeball to a flock of braver-than-most seagulls in an alley, fighting over a corn chip: kitten. They are very cute, and cute can get you killed.

16. The energy that surrounded Coach could not be dismissed among the girls and boys; it got hold of you from the inside out like a drumbeat stuck in your head: sex.

Ground Fighting

speranza and some of the old softball team were at the taco shack, so I gave them a head nod. They did the same. I missed her. The fries and tacos are made-to-order, so it takes for-goddamn-ever. Except for the one time Esperanza came to visit me in the hospital, we weren't ever really friends. Poly High in Long Beach looked like a commercial for a PG-13 teen dramedy full of colorful faces and the scent of coastal California: special episodes for the homeless epidemic, rampant STDs, minor race wars, and socioeconomic inequality.

Esperanza liked to be weird and mysterious. She was into Care Bears, alien conspiracies, and watching men sting themselves with the world's most toxic insects online, so her behavior made sense at the time. She had heavy black hair, wore V-neck T-shirts unraveling at the hems. Her eyes fell too deeply in her skull so she always looked skeletal in photographs. Still, a V-neck is the opposite of secrecy, so I thought I knew everything but was still surprised in the end.

I'm not sure if it's obvious, but I'm not that into people. A person is fine. Sometimes a person is fine, but people are a problem. They're loud and have a lot to say that usually doesn't add up, and it's confusing. Then I realize they're confused and to explain it all would be a lot of energy best left for anything else.

At the taco stand I make eye contact with objects, the gum streaks on the concrete like acne scars, lots of shoes, the sparrows ticking their heads to get a view of fallen scraps one eye at a time. Esperanza has a picture of a red-haired white woman on a key chain swinging from her backpack. The woman looks severe but knowing and wears a black blazer. I assumed she must be a singer from some blazer-wearing Swedish pop band.

The girls feigned interest in the boys' conversations about people with unique abilities, how some humans have not evolved and still have prehistoric tendons that allow them to climb better than others. I knew the stories the girls would tell later when the boys were gone, whose dick had skin tags, how to get Vicodin for really bad cramps or just how to get Vicodin, or how one girl's boyfriend always fingered her till she bled. Every time. The girls usually pretended to listen but found this particular conversation interesting enough to begin checking out each other's hands. I found a good spot to stand alone and wait for my order. All the voices and conversation began to muffle into chirps no different than birds organizing their day from the tops of trees. I started to imagine Esperanza dancing to weird accents and Irish crooning in her bedroom among all the hip-hop and mariachi that thrums in our neighborhood and smiled to myself like an idiot.

"You think that's funny?"

A random boy appeared in front of me and repeated the question. I recognized him. He played junior varsity basketball and baseball. I asked what was happening because I sincerely wasn't paying attention. Then I felt Esperanza grab my wrist and pull it to her face.

"She's the one!" Esperanza yelled.

My former teammates cheered and started clearing off a table. The boy sat down on one side, and put his arm up for a wrestling match.

"Me?"

"It's bullshit," Esperanza whispered, "but you can beat that fool without trying."

Another of the boys eyed my wrists and hands, then my whole body.

"I don't know, man," he said, "she looks like she could kick a door down."

Esperanza cursed and ushered me to the seat. I mentioned that I just wanted my fries and no one listened. I didn't bother mentioning I was grieving a lost parent and just had surgery on my elbow two months ago. If they didn't care about food, they wouldn't care about that. My father believed in sports the way he believed in the weather; they guided our days, and we adjusted our whole lives to the games. Without him I lost my faith in balls and sticks.

JV Boy's hand looked relatively clean, but I still didn't care to touch it, let alone hold it tightly for several seconds or more. I looked up at Esperanza. She was nearly taller than everybody, even the teachers. I wanted to give her my pocket change and take her places and erase all the other heads, even the ladies making the orders in the tiny hot kitchen behind the counter. I wondered if love begins that way, hoping to erase other people's bodies.

I grabbed JV Boy's palm and held it tight.

"First, we test the grip," he said.

I felt him try to move my hand back by the wrist, so I tightened instinctively in resistance. His own hand moved back easily, so I rotated the whole thing so his knuckles faced my chin.

"Oh shit," he said.

Someone counted to three. The pressure engaged. He dug his jagged nails into my skin and shook the table a little. My bare elbow on the wood felt grated and stung. Pain, to me, is a portal, an access point to another world, the smallest of places and those infinite in scale. When I broke my arm, I went to the atoms. When I buried my father, I went to the stars. When I came out to my mother, she told me to wash my hair, then I went to the past. It's the greatest high when your own body is so wrecked you get to leave it for a while. With his hand in that position he had no chance to win. All I had to do was endure the pinch, the pressure, the sting, then pull his arm a little farther out and it was over. I won. The screaming was incredible. The boys, the girls, the little ladies in the kitchen giggled like something extraordinary had happened.

"She swoll. She swoll!" the boys chanted.

"Fucking man is what she is," JV lamented, and demanded a rematch.

At that last declaration I felt a different kind of hurt, familiar and wicked. I ignored it and the others ignored it, the suggestion that something about my body was not quite right. But there was a hot and sexy bag of fries on the counter with my number on it. I took them and walked away. The skies in Southern California are beautiful in the early evening. The smog ignites in gold and fuchsia. I wasn't diagnosed as intersex until twelve, more female than male so before that girl was just a good guess. After a few paces I felt I wasn't alone. Then I wasn't alone. Esperanza followed me. We said, "Hey," one after the other.

It was quiet for a while but not a bad kind. She apologized for making me arm wrestle, but I told her it was fun. She was surprised I wasn't hurt by what JV had said. There was more of that good quiet. I offered her some fries, meaning my heart, my blood, my future. She declined, said she had already eaten.

"Who is that lady on your backpack?"

"What?"

"On the key chain?"

"Scully?"

I had no clue, but turns out the woman was not a Euro-pop superstar but instead an actress named Gillian Anderson, star of *The X-Files*. All of which I knew nothing about and all of which Esperanza was now determined to explain in full. I liked listening to her talk, her head above me framed in the pink clouds.

When I first met Esperanza a year ago we were gathering on the softball field for the first practice. The other

girls laughed, tossed balls at each other, or scrunched their
eyes into the sun for the pain of it. Esperanza walked over
to me with an agenda. She looked like she was going to
give me a hug or punch me in the mouth. Whatever it
was would be too much, and I lost my breath. Instead she
just pivoted on her heel and stood next to me, not saying
anything at all. The movement of her chest reminded me
that I needed to breathe, so I did and thankfully avoided
passing out like a dumbass. Before she came over I didn't
realize how scary it was to be there with those strange
girls and the ribbons and the rules I barely knew yet of
how to pay attention but not stare, how to walk like them
and love their walk, how to recognize the pack, be strong
but not too strong, be satisfied with stepping aside for
boys, how disappointment would be a condition of life,
how being a girl can take the air out of our lungs before
we have a chance to protest. But with Esperanza suddenly
and fiercely at my side for no other reason than it seemed
right, I felt claimed. I felt happy.

After the arm wrestling, Esperanza asked if she could
come over to my house. Before my dad died that was normal. He hosted parties for the team. They loved him way
more than me. I wanted to tell her that my house wasn't
the same house now, but looked up into the shadows of her
eyes and got lost in a stuttering yes. I thought Esperanza
and I were going to hang out together, alone at my house,
for the first time, and chill (not start fucking at random),
just relax without me plugged up to an IV and constipated
from surgery after my elbow was shattered by a fastball.

It was still early in the evening and my house was empty. It was a two-bedroom off Pine with no parking. Esperanza flopped on the couch like it was hers, and I couldn't help but smile. It had been hard to recognize my house since the funeral and now more so with Esperanza's whole body in it. It was a nice room, with a faux-suede sectional, warm sunlight, and a checkered rug. Happy people could've lived there. I sat on the edge beside her, then sank a little deeper, then back to the edge again. Esperanza laughed.

"You're so girly," she said. "Let me see your laptop."

I obeyed. Then we started talking about nipples and I was less nervous. We had for-real nipple talk, the whole science of it after some online videos' algorithm diverted us too far in one direction. Or we did it to ourselves. After accidentally/on purpose committing twenty-seven minutes to amateur porn, we had vast theories. Tiny nipples always indicate confidence, imminent success, conqueror of huge cocks, summoner of orgasms, with total disregard for the pleasure of anyone but herself. The big tits are shy at first, then wildly dominant to the point of alarm. Still, all of it can change depending on the direction they point. There is no argument against nipples and fate. Esperanza simply declared that I was into tits and asked me for something to drink. I got her sparkling water.

"Why don't you like your house?" she asked like a therapist being paid by the hour. I got warm and felt like too much of me had been seen without my permission, as if the truth of my whole life stuffed down deep had been squirming around on the floor this whole time. I told her I don't like being at home anymore. That wasn't good enough, so I told her more.

"I came out to my mom, and she looked at me, looked at my forehead really, looked hard like it was either missing or communicating better than my own voice. Then she looked up even higher and told me to wash my hair. That's all."

Esperanza drank from her can and swallowed with difficulty, then burped unceremoniously and apologized in a whisper. She didn't ask me about my mother again and just put on some videos of baby elephants being rescued from muddy ditches. It helped.

The first time I had a wet dream about Esperanza we were on a beach because I thought that's where people do that kind of thing, sugar themselves with sand and salt, grinding to the rhythm of the waves or some shit. The dream ended like a dropped water balloon, and I had a slightly harder time looking Esperanza in the face for about a day. Then it passed. At the end of the third and fifth wet dreams Esperanza shouldered through my bedroom door in a pantsuit and a roid rage, then shot me in the chest with an FBI standard-issue nine-millimeter.

After the arm-wrestling night, she came over the next day to take me somewhere. She told me to wear sweats. I thought we might go for a run along the beach through the houses we probably wouldn't ever afford and drop candy wrappers in their flower gardens. Instead, we ended up in the dank back room of a gym/donut shop on Magnolia

Ave. doing Brazilian jiujitsu. Magnolia Ave. ropes its way through a business district full of warehouses and multi-purpose buildings. The gym could've once been anything from an ice-cream storage facility to a craft-beer brewery. An American flag and a flag of the Philippines sagged on the wall high up in the air, photos of Filipino fighters in shiny shorts posed, muscles taut in preparation to do harm for eternity. All along the wall were punching bags—a black one with duct tape, a brand-new red one, and one shaped like the upper half of a Band-Aid-colored man. The gym had to be two stories, a couple thousand square feet, the only enclosed space was a tiny bathroom I smelled right away, a very unventilated fecal aroma, while the rest carried a familiar sweaty scent, staleness, a faint lemon-scented disinfectant, and something distinctly male. Past lives from previous tenants still haunted the room via boxes piled in the corner, haphazard mats thrown on the floor, and the banners hung up on ropes instead of fastened to the wall. Gouges of paint and plaster from other built-in structures that had been removed cascaded along the wall's surface as if all of it could be sucked out at any moment and grow something else instead, some other temporary dream. I didn't feel like working out or sweating or kickboxing. We'd gone off plan, a plan I hadn't gotten around to verbalizing, of course, but the plan nonetheless.

This is my cousin Sensei Reyes, Esperanza said.

Sensei Reyes had fighter coming off him like fog, at least twice our age with a bald head like a raptor in a washed-out blue gi. Esperanza was taller than him by a lot. He had a short neck, short legs, and dense rack-of-beef back. They had the same thick eyebrows, though he was much darker and kind of happier, the way some people always seem to have a song or joke replaying in their heads.

A woman came out of the hallway, bringing with her the smell of butter, sugar, and her own pleasant fragrance that was everything the room was not. Black hair hung to her ass. A little girl popped from behind with pink frosting splattered down her shirt and around her face, as if she had thrown her whole head into a pile of cupcakes and shaken it. The girl skipped over to the Band-Aid-colored torso punching-bag man and began to climb him.

"Get down, Ana."

The girl protested and frowned for the first time.

"But I love him," Ana pleaded.

The real class began to trickle in. Aging men with youthful hopes of being champion mixed-martial-arts fighters or just not being bullied. They ignored me and Esperanza, as far as I could tell, which felt nice. Two women came in too, one a colorful older lady in peacock yoga pants and the other not. The other woman was so thin and timid that she almost disappeared entirely whenever she turned sideways. Sensei Reyes had us run in circles, taking turns punching the Band-Aid man, which I'm sure he thought was a grand gesture of feminist solidarity. I liked him for it. Then we did some extra weird shit. He made us pair up, get on the ground, and practice untangling our legs from one another while trying to trap the other person. It was confusing as hell. I got paired with the yoga pants lady and thought this was all wrong.

The coast I knew in Long Beach had soiled baby diapers, needle caps, condoms, and too many seaweed pods to walk on barefoot. It was beautiful like it was supposed to be in pictures far away, but not enough to peel your body out and roll around in. That would be stupid. I didn't need to be killed in a dream over and over to know that Esperanza was a sexual threat. She ate sherbet, orange, had her phone programmed with start times of cable cartoon-channel season premieres, never had a pet, put lip gloss on right after eating, never ironed her softball uniform, always had tiny crushed bags of chips in her backpack for "emergencies," liked to put me in dangerous situations for unspecified reasons, and could possibly be very, very straight just like little Ana and her lover Band-Aid Man.

"You're just supposed to use leg," Sensei Reyes told me. "That comes later."

He pulled my hands off the old woman's knees because I kept trying to reposition her. Esperanza was paired up with the two-dimensional woman while I had to slide my legs along a menopausal white lady's yoga pants like we were two monstrous crickets wondering what the hell happened to the day. I wanted to be with Esperanza, though with this much contact I might've passed out. The point of it all had vanished. Where there was an intention to knead the afternoon into brilliance, roll it all up into something nice and warm like Christmas lights, I ended up knotted against a strange woman like we were mushed meat and bone all together and still by ourselves.

And then Esperanza was gone completely. I didn't know it the first day. She didn't text me that day and didn't show up to school or jiujitsu. The absence hurt. I was paired up with Noemi. Turns out the mousy timid woman who seemed dangerous as a lukewarm glass of water could put a submission hold on you that would lift your ghost to the ceiling. I remembered a party at my house with the team. No parents, no rules, just thin walls between us and the next town house, so everybody kept it reasonable. We were athletes and really good and had practice in the morning, so no one got that high. Instead, we watched porn. Watching porn with softball players is like watching a horror movie or a documentary. Most of them looked at it like they were reading an instruction manual, the rest of us were mortified at the human species as a whole. We sought out the most absurd videos that had the best user approval rating, but ultimately no matter the context of the video, eventually a penis of substantial girth went into a neat and pulsing vagina. I knew that experience would never be me, how my own body seemed too far away from the veiny dicks or carefully folded labia. The moment before the sex when the pair still talked, still had a way in or out and still considered their future, I felt an almost-arousal, my underwear sliding against me, my body wakening real and firm as a knuckle. Then it went away. The videos clicked on and on from hairy to waxed, to messy in a controlled way then not a controlled way, to artificial sound effects of liquid sloshing, to a total absence of faces and wrists and knees, leaving nothing but sections of bodies carved out for the thrum of feeling they provided without the troubling business of life before or after that singular moment. I felt sorry for everyone involved.

When Esperanza was gone for a week, three other guys came in to jiujitsu class, all of them teenagers like me and Esperanza, but not at all like me and Esperanza. I recognized their faces but never spoke to them or knew their names. One had adenoids and a whole lot to say even though he couldn't breathe through his nose. Another had a skin condition that caused a kind of moldy crust to form at his joints. The last one was big, musky, queer, and would become my favorite. It was the saddest bunch of losers.

They smelled like boys, meaning they smelled like wet puppies—metallic and peppery, with a dash of mildew. They weren't like me and Esperanza at all. We had hard shoulders and jaws. We did the exercises as if they would never end because that's what we were used to, practice had no final count. Everything began again and again to tear down our muscles for them to rebuild. The class had to run around the building four times before we could start. I ran full-out for five minutes and lapped them all twice. I thought my heart would explode when I finally stopped. When it didn't I just laughed. No one else laughed even though it was funny to be so alive just then. They were afraid of me. I liked it. Sensei looked at me when he announced a tournament with the wave of a black-and-white flyer. I just stretched and tried not to think about her. Adenoids asked me what kind of stretches I was doing, and if I was sure that would be good for jiujitsu. I told him any stretch is a good stretch, and the words came out so smooth and convincing it should've been etched on a rock and made a religion. He nodded and imitated my movement; then they all did. I had never experienced anything like it. They weren't used to winning, and I could tell. The softball team were champions (near-champions, at least). We'd gone to regionals every year. I felt like this bunch would never make it past a certificate of participation. The thing I knew for sure was I could do anything I wanted here.

The next day, still no Esperanza. I thought she was dead. She's dead. She died. Died. Died. Dead and done, I told myself. I'd rather her be alive than dead, but dead rather than an asshole. Sensei paired me up with Reginald, the big softy, and left the dojo for a while. When he came back in, he screamed.

"It's not football!"

I'd been taking turns shoulder-ramming all three of the losers one at a time. Reginald was fun to push. He looked jiggly but was pretty solid and giggled a lot if I grabbed him by the man tit.

"She cheats, Mr. Sensei," Reginald panted. "Nips are off-limits."

"I don't care about your breasts."

Sensei Reyes turned red at his own words, at the reality

of his new students, but kept talking without a quiver in his aging voice. Adenoids fell on his ass in silent laughter, not recovering in time to get any other instructions. I was small here, and it felt strange not to have the most powerful legs and arms. I didn't know if I liked that yet or if it was worth the missed after-school pizza comas at home.

"Get in bottom position."

Reginald obeyed, fake-wincing at pain in his left tit. Sensei took top position behind and said, "This is good," his two hands held together like the logo of a youth center. Even though Reginald was a buffalo, I could still rotate him around with some effort. He, however, seemed completely shocked that he could not pin me with ease. I had no idea what was legal or illegal, technique or flight response. Reginald yelled that I was cheating again. Sensei told him to shut up and fight. The tone was familiar to me now, and I knew exactly where I was again. Sensei wasn't red anymore, never left during warm-ups because something new had sprouted, and in that moment he sensed glory was not just possible but likely.

After practice my muscles shook and my skin felt rubbed raw like paper under an eraser. It was good. Then Adenoids asked me if I was gay and if I had a dick. I hit him in the throat. Reginald fell down ass-first laughing, but I helped Adenoids get on his feet anyway. That was pretty much how we said hello and goodbye. We were cool.

Two weeks passed without hearing from Esperanza, and I'd mourned her by losing six pounds plus gaining a basket of bruises and scratches from anyone and anything Sensei put in front of me. People think emotions are what separate us from the animals, but they're wrong. It's winning (and thumbs) that make our species nearer to God than ordinary beasts. The stakes might be high or low or nonexistent, but victory and defeat are everything. Competition inspires improvement. We make better food, superior tools, gain insight, develop the art of strategy, wage war, topple empires, invent prejudices, form tribes, implement branding to enable us to fight, cut, kill, and defeat. It's also really fun. Without competition we stop moving, and I'd rather be dead than stand still forever. I forget all the times I poured salt on snails just to watch them bubble up into hot soup. There was something primal, intentional, mystical about that—a life for a wish, a summoning of something dark and old. Glancing at Esperanza was wonderful and cruel like pouring salt on a snail, but I couldn't tell if she looked at me like that with intention or by accident. To just take a life on accident seemed like a different kind of mysticism, a poorly timed joke from small-headed gods reminding us that nothing is in our control, especially death and love.

I found out Esperanza wasn't dead or cruel, just sick. Sensei Reyes paired me that day with Noemi, who put me in an arm bar eleven times before I bit her. After I bit Noemi out of loneliness and desperation, she seemed to think we'd become bonded somehow and started telling me her life story and national statistics for violent crime. I struggled to keep her forearm from sinking in around my throat while she said she dropped out of college because her chemistry professor was a sexual predator. She went to art school later.

"Nine out of ten women experience some degree of sexual assault in a lifetime," Noemi said, putting the squeeze on me even harder.

She was two-thirds of my weight, twice my age, all bones and muscle like a skinless chicken on steroids. I finally got free, only for us to start all over again.

"This used to be my only stress relief," Noemi continued while wrapping her legs around my waist and crushing me tight. "Now I draw cat heads for people."

I tapped out. She let me go.

"Cat heads?"

"Cat heads. Heads of peoples' cats. Custom jobs. They pay like forty to fifty dollars each. People love their cats more than other people sometimes, or themselves. Cats are like the best of us. I'll send you the link."

I almost said that all cats look alike, but I didn't because Noemi would probably think that was racist. I just nodded and finally surprised Noemi with a takedown. She giggled like it was the funniest joke ever, and I knew she'd gone crazy a long time ago but was fine with that. With my arm pulled to near-point-of-break in the vise of Noemi's whole body, I believed Esperanza's claim of me meant a promise, an understanding of our whole selves.

I only joined the class for Esperanza, even though she technically never asked me, never gave me a real choice, just led me there and suddenly I was staving off choke holds and grappling barefoot in a poorly air-conditioned warehouse. Maybe it was a gift, this personal, physical thing she did with her family. Maybe it was nothing. I went to her house and knocked on the front door for the first time to check on her. You never really know a person until you see their house, where they keep their eggs and take all their shits. That's how you can tell if their soul is broken or locked up tight or sitting at that perfect Gold-ilocks temperature of well-adjusted human being. When we were teammates Esperanza seemed at odds with her own body, like she wanted it to do things it had no interest in. When we had no team I knew we might be friends, might be more, but her grandmother answered the door, and I realized I knew nothing at all. The door opened and a wave of dust slid over my face. Skillets. Unopened Bar-bie doll boxes. Two dozen cans of mosquito repellent. Chairs stacked high to the ceiling, useful as a sculpture made of butter in a rainstorm. Magazines piled so dense and high their spines looked like thread in a tapestry. Tiki torches. Remote-control cars. Posters rolled up. *Star Wars* collector's edition mugs. Candles of the Madonna in frag-ile rows like a carnival game. Little green baskets that once held berries: emptied. Garden hoses. PVC piping. Mattress foam stacked like pastries. Military-grade ration packages, hollowed/consumed. A box of tire irons. Board games probably missing pieces. Lampshades. Everything. There was everything in that house.

"She's got mono," her grandmother said, "sleeping it off. We can wake her up."

She pulled a tissue from her apron pocket and blew her nose like a tuba.

I didn't know Esperanza was being raised by her grandmother. I didn't know she had no parents in a wholly acceptable way. I had no parents because one was dead and the other was, well, I didn't know what to call Mama then other than high. Grief is like that; it walks upright sometimes and crawls slowly for other people.

I looked up symptoms of mononucleosis, aka the kissing disease, which include fever, sore throat, and fatigue for weeks. It is often caused by the Epstein-Barr virus, which can result in cognitive impairment over long periods of time. I wondered if that meant she would forget my name, my face, and the rest. I told Esperanza's grandmother not to bother her and turned away. Esperanza had avoided me so I wouldn't visit. She didn't want me to see her house for a fairly good reason. There was a lot to see. I should've texted like a normal person, but I was angry and impatient and ready to forget her if I had to. After seeing the house, I figured she'd want me to forget her, forget their densely packed archive of advertisements, dolls, and all the other remnants of human garbage / memory.

It was safe to assume Esperanza had been tonguekissing a bunch of people from school and her church, though we'd never kissed. She'd been hiding from me. I apologized to her grandmother and told her to forget about it. I didn't bother responding to Esperanza once she started feeling better and texting again.

On the day of the tournament something strange happened. A lot of people came to see us. It was at a gymnasium, brightly lit and clean. The different dojos sold merchandise at tables. They made it look easy and safe and people signed up their children for sample lessons. A big part of being any good at sports is just acceptance, working very hard to be uncomfortable and living through it.

My first challenger was from Hawaiian Gardens, Samoan, and skinny. He wanted to win. I appreciated that but knew he didn't understand how much he would have to give up. We started in neutral where anything is possible, both of us standing in front of each other with arms open.

I was up two points and in bottom position. He scooted behind me and tried to grind his head into my shoulders, push hard against my bones nearest to the surface of my skin. I had to accept the pain he gave and not be moved by it, not shift my hands to avoid it, not bend my legs to deny it. Let it happen and hold.

The hard plastic of his helmet pressed into the bony part of my neck. It would bruise and tear like dropped fruit. I was fine. I went to the future. Esperanza and I didn't have names for each other, but someday we might. Someday is a place where the lost and the dead come back to us, where promises happen on the hour and the impossible sits on windowsills to be petted and fed. My opponent was in an arm bar and didn't want to break a limb, didn't want to feel the strain in his hamstrings from his foot wedged under his body. It's not about wanting the pain, and if he could accept it for just a little longer until the timer ran out he could start over and try again.

When I looked to the crowd and didn't see anyone I knew at all, I went to a highway in a desert I'd never seen, in a car I didn't own yet with someone I knew I loved asleep in the passenger seat. It wasn't a big crowd and there were no flags or painted faces or pom-poms. I thought about letting him go, giving him another chance to win in a world of losses, but that thought didn't last long. I didn't go to the future or the past and pulled hard enough to hear a scream and feel the tap of surrender against the mat. The crowd began to cheer. Their feet made the floor quake just a little, and I didn't leave. I stayed there.

Then she was back. Esperanza was fully recovered and back at school and jiujitsu class, I couldn't ignore her anymore. I didn't have the words to say that I understood that we were impossible, that we didn't fit together, so I didn't say anything. She walked over to me past the punching bags and I had an instant urge to hide behind one but held my ground. I knew that walk, the one with purpose, the one that said she would bottle me up or destroy me and nothing in between.

"Can you come to my house tonight?" she asked.

As if no time had passed at all, I gave her a sad yes cracked around the edges and felt stupid. Sensei ordered us to run around the building. During sparring I had to give Noemi back to Esperanza. The three of us were the only women left in the class except for the occasional trial sample attendant who never lasted more than two visits. Sensei let me work on kicks via Band-Aid Man for the sparring session. I kicked it so hard the neck tore open, a gash of yellow foam revealing itself. I quickly held the head back in place in a slight panic, worried for little Ana, thinking I'd killed her best friend or her lover or her daddy, then remembered he wasn't real. No one was hurt more than usual. I did front kicks to the sternum just to be safe.

Esperanza didn't talk all practice after confirming I would go to her house. In silence we rode our bikes back, her heavy eyebrows low and serious. Not saying things in the evening was our thing, but this was thicker. We were mad at each other.

Right as we approached her house she nearly veered her bike into mine. Her eyes were invisible in the hollows of her face like always, but there was something else. I'd seen the inside of her home on accident. I'd seen the piles and piles of useless garbage, the musky smell of incarcerated time, cardboard, and insects. People who lose their most valuable possessions will start to collect all things trivial as a substitute. I didn't know what Esperanza's grandmother had lost. Esperanza found shame in it all, and that made me very angry. I wanted to hate her for hating her house and I think I managed to do it, hate her for just a minute.

She announced herself to her grandma by shouting up at the ceiling, sending the sound over the columns of junk. Her grandma shouted back an acknowledgment, then sneezed like a soprano from her bedroom, a scream in the shadows.

I wanted to grab Esperanza and throw her down and pick her up and throw her down again, yank at her bones and twist them in, make her my height and even smaller, collapse her skin and muscle into light and press it into my chest, keep her there with nothing to do but bang against my ribs to remind me that I still had her for as long as I could stand it.

We went to her room, both tired, she more than me, and the buzzing of endorphins and the hurt of being ignored in a way that I wasn't entitled to left me almost high. She hugged me. Esperanza Duarte put her arms around me and held me to her like we hadn't seen each other for years and had been waiting for this day. I felt her ear slide against mine and her breath on my shoulder from above. It was a long hug. When she let me go I thought I might pop like a soap bubble, but I stayed whole and she just sat down on her bed. I could see the tiredness from being sick for so many weeks and suddenly working out again, but she smiled and made room for me. Her legs stuck out inches past mine and she pulled a protein bar out of what seemed to be the air and started munching. After I laughed, she offered me one. We ate them together, staring at the ceiling fan. Not long after, she got halfway under the covers next to me, then motioned for me to do the same. I had on my street clothes, but she didn't care. The lights were on and her grandma's allergies kept kicking up in the next room. I had lied to Esperanza when I said my mother told me to wash my hair after coming out. More came after. "You can't be gay," she told me. "Either way, you can't be gay." She said it like a joke, like the idea of me was so preposterous, as if being intersex meant that I did not belong to any other idea at all, as if I weren't really there, just a cartoon pig or a toy on a shelf. Half-amused and half-terrified, she turned away from me, and then that truly was all.

I hadn't put much thought into how bodies are supposed to love each other. Maybe we had been lovers all that time, and I didn't recognize it. We'd grappled in class, held each other down, tugged at our joints to the brink of the unbearable.

Esperanza took off her pants and underwear from beneath the covers so I couldn't see anything. Then she slid her legs around me sideways. I lay there for her, flat, still fully clothed for a while, then she tugged everything off of me. Esperanza didn't touch me like I was an anomaly but like I was a memory, a place she'd forgotten and missed deeply. It felt like being wrapped in hot dough, then boiled alive. She shuddered and stopped moving, the salty sweat from her head and mouth warm against my neck. When things hurt me, time opens up and shatters, but this was the opposite, this was being pitched through the universe and back, violent and swift without any pain at all.

Acknowledgments

Many thanks to all my teachers—those intentional, occasional, and accidental—for your inspiration, especially to those who threw erasers at me for flapping in class. My agent, Jin Auh, deserves hefty bags of gratitude for being such a sharp, dangerous treasure. Thank you to Emily Bell for selecting this collection and being such a boss, along with Jackson, Sean, and the team at MCD. Thanks to my Fresno fam, including Roman Wilkey, Ginny Barnes, and Romaine Desclos, for providing such queer feminine chaos energy. Thank you, Joseph Cassara, Brynn Saito, and my extended family of colleagues and friends, for walking with me (literally, on my writing rants through the park). All kinds of love to my Live, Write crew—Ros, Greg, Jia, Jen, and Lorissa—for reminding me that people all over the place care about words. Thanks to my brothers, Donald Blackburn and Derek Blackburn, as well as my nieces, Iyanna, Kennedi, and Kendall, for providing lots of content (smile and wink), and my beautiful aunts, especially Susie Green and Venissa Horrington, who have supported me in both writing and survival in this wild world.